29

THE GIRLS OF CANBY HALL

A ROOMMATE RETURNS

EMILY CHASE

SCHOLASTIC INC.
New York Toronto London Auckland Sydney

In memory of Jessica Berman

ISBN 0-590-41671-5

12 11 10 9 8 7 6 5 4 3 2 1 7 8 9/8 0 1 2/9

Printed in the U.S.A. 01

First Scholastic printing, August 1988

29

THE GIRLS OF CANBY HALL

A ROOMMATE RETURNS

29

THE GIRLS OF CANBY HALL

Roommates
Our Roommate Is Missing
You're No Friend of Mine
Keeping Secrets
Summer Blues
Best Friends Forever
Four Is a Crowd
The Big Crush
Boy Trouble
Make Me a Star
With Friends Like That
Who's the New Girl?
Here Come the Boys
What's a Girl To Do?
To Tell the Truth
Three of a Kind
Graduation Day
Making Friends
One Boy Too Many
Something Old, Something New
Friends Times Three
Party Time!
Troublemaker
The Almost Summer Carnival
But She's So Cute
Princess Who?
The Ghost of Canby Hall
Help Wanted!
The Roommate and the Cowboy
Happy Birthday, Jane
A Roommate Returns

Chapter One

Autumn streamed through the window of Room 407, Baker House, Canby Hall, sending a hard, butter-yellow sunlight exactly on the spot where Andrea Cord, Jane Barrett, and Toby Houston were finishing off a big Sunday midday eat-in with the contents of the latest CARE package from Andy's mother and father.

Andy always shared the lavish shipments of food her parents sent regularly from their restaurant in Chicago. Making a whole meal from it was not exactly usual, ". . . but sometimes I just can't stand the thought of another dining hall meal," Jane sighed, laying thick strips of cheese on a bagel.

The roommates were gathered around the footlocker-table, which Jane had covered with a pink, flowered bedsheet. A pretty sheet used as a tablecloth was one of those things Toby called real Jane. Jane also was sitting real

Jane, neatly cross-legged, her long blonde hair falling over her right eye, her favorite blue housecoat properly buttoned up. Toby, redheaded, in jeans, a denim shirt, and boots, was hunkered down on her heels like the Texas ranch hands she grew up among. It was a way of sitting that still amazed her city-bred roommates, but for Toby it was as comfortable and homelike as being on a horse.

Andy, of course, was sitting up straight and gracefully, as though she couldn't sit any other way, and was nibbling the last of a lemon cookie. With a soft smile on her face, she realized she was feeling terrifically happy. This semester her schedule worked out so she could take two ballet classes a week, including an advanced class which she loved; and the night before she and her boyfriend Matt had gone to a movie and then walked and talked and walked and talked for hours.

"I definitely think," she said, looking down at the assorted foods laid out, "that when someone in my family works out a way to send piping hot ribs through the post office, life will be practically perfect."

"I promise when they manage to send them, I'll eat them," Toby said.

Andy raised her upper body, bent over her long legs in a dancer's stretch, then slowly straightened up. "Anybody for a movie this afternoon?" she asked. "*White Nights* is playing in Greenleaf."

"How many times have you seen that already?" Jane wanted to know.

Andy laughed. "A hundred times wouldn't be enough," she answered. "Baryshnikov *and* Gregory Hines." There was no question that Andrea Cord was addicted to dancing and dancers.

"Sorry, I'm taking Maxine out," Toby said. She glanced at her watch. "Got to get going soon, too. It's a pretty day, and I don't want to miss it." Maxine was a spirited brown mare that Randy Crowell kept on his farm and let Toby ride whenever she wanted to.

"I wish it were raining instead of pretty outside," Jane said mournfully. "I'm going to be stuck inside all day with geometry."

She glanced over at her desk, covered with books, papers, and a couple of sweaters, and shrugged. "Why do I always have a load of math homework to do on Sunday?"

"Because you don't do it on Friday or Saturday," Toby explained, taking the last bite of her sliced ham-from-a-can and peanut butter sandwich, a combo she had invented.

"Something like that," Jane sadly agreed.

Suddenly they heard a new, unexpected voice.

"This is so hard to believe," it exclaimed. "We used to do *exactly* the same thing."

Surprised, the girls looked up and saw a slightly familiar, pretty blonde, older girl standing in the doorway, smiling down at them. Her fresh face with its bright blue eyes was topped by curly hair, and she was wearing very, *very* bright orange pants and matching long sweater and loop earrings that dangled almost to her shoulders. Andy, the most fashion-smart of the three roommates, instantly decided that the *idea* of the girl's outfit was terrific, but it didn't exactly work out right. A second later, her eyes lit up.

"Why, it's Shelley Hyde!" she exclaimed. "Come on in!"

"Are you *pozz?* I don't want to disturb you."

Then Toby and Jane recognized her, too. Shelley was a former 407-er. Jane, Toby, and Andy had inherited the room after Shelley and her roommates graduated from Canby Hall. The six roommates, past and present, had spent a few days together the year before, when Alison Cavanaugh, the popular Baker House housemother, had her wedding at Canby Hall, and the older girls came back from college for it.

The girls got up, Andy in one quick graceful movement, Toby smiling her engaging grin, and Jane looking rather regal. They remembered Shelley very well. She had been a drama student at her college, and the theatrical style she added to some of the naive funny stories she told about the old days at Canby Hall had made them roll over laughing.

Now Shelley *swooped* through the doorway.

"Hi, ya, girls," she said. Then she stopped

just where she was and stood gazing around.

"Oh, the memories I have of this room! You'll understand what I mean after you graduate and go on to college and all that. I mean, you just never forget, oh, you know, the room and the times you had in it and your friends, your special forever Canby Hall friends. Do you mind if I just feast my eyes for a sec?"

"Sure, walk around. *Mi casa es su casa.* We learned that in Spanish. It means, My house is your house," Jane said.

"Help yourself," Toby added with a smile and a wave of her hand.

"Thanks a mil," Shelley said and, as the girls stood back, began a slow circle around the room. She ran her fingers along the wall.

"Pretty blue walls. I forgot you painted the walls blue. It's real pretty" — she reached a window and her fingers touched the pane — "but no stack of cans on the window sill, I notice. We always had a pyramid of diet soda on this window right here." Turning, she looked up to the ceiling. "Oh, it's still here. . . ." She peered intently. "Has the meaning of it been revealed?"

The girls were silent. It was Toby's tea bag, fastened to the ceiling above her bed; no one knew why and Toby never would tell.

"Um . . . Oh, I love this look," she said, moving on along, patting the modern print cover in warm earth tones that was on Andy's bed. She noticed Andy's carefully framed posters of ballet dancers up on the wall behind the bed. "Oh, sure, I remember. This is yours, Andy. Last year you wanted to be a dancer."

"I still do," Andy said. "My aim in life is to be a great ballerina."

Shelley turned from the posters to Andy.

"Good for you," she said. "It's important to have a goal. I know. I've had one since Canby Hall, just like you. The important thing is to keep your goal in front of you all the time. That's what I've done, and here I am on my way to reaching it. If you have a goal, don't give it up. Promise you won't!"

Andy grinned. "I promise," she said. She had decided to dedicate herself to becoming a dancer long before Canby Hall, after her very first ballet class. She didn't intend for a second to give up her ambition.

But the grin faded as she watched Shelley turn and go back to moving around the room. Neat and tidy herself, Andy wished for the millionth time that Jane would just once clean up the mess that was her third of the room. Jane Barrett, of the old society Boston Barretts, was a victim of a lifetime of maids and other servants; to the irritation of her roommates, she acted as if she were incapable of hanging up, folding up, placing on shelves, or in any other way putting anything away. She always simply tossed things in a heap on her bed, chair, desk, and floor.

"Come on over and have some of the Cord family restaurant's finest," Andy said, wanting — even though she knew it was silly — to divert Shelley from Jane's messiness.

"Oh, I shouldn't," Shelley said with an embarrassed smile as she immediately stopped her tour. "I'm supposed to be worrying about my weight."

But she came over, studied the food, and picked up a chocolate doughnut. She looked as though she were going to eat it, but instead, to her own surprise, all she did was hold it.

"If you knew me better, you'd never believe this. I don't believe it myself." She looked at them with her eyes wide. "I can't eat," she said. "I guess I'm too excited."

"Too excited at seeing Room 407?" Toby asked in disbelief.

Shelley laughed.

"Not exactly. It's something else," she admitted.

Andy cocked her head and gave Shelley a long probing look. "Do you tell us?" she asked.

With that, Shelley settled down on the floor as though she were going to stay forever.

"I sure do. It's the most exciting thing that ever happened to me," she said. She looked into one, then the other, then the third face. Toby's grin came on again at Shelley's next gestures, a run of both hands through her curly hair, and then a glance down, as though shy, and after that, a strong upward thrust of her chin. Toby thought Shelley was putting on a pretty good act, but she was sure that it *was* an act. Shelley's next words confirmed it.

"Tomorrow is the first day of the beginning of my life," Shelley said.

Toby didn't have an idea what that could mean. She flashed a quizzical frown to Jane, but Jane was simply looking politely attentive.

"I guess it sounds foolish," Shelley said. "But I don't mean it to. It's that tomorrow is my first day as a professional actress. Tomorrow I start rehearsals in the new play at The Center Stage Theater in Boston."

"Hey," Andy said. "That's terrific."

"Congratulations, Shelley," Jane said, and Toby added a sound that also could have meant congratulations.

"Yes," Shelley agreed with such open delight that the girls all smiled at her. "It's as though my whole life begins tomorrow at ten in the morning."

"That's really so great, Shelley," Andy said.

Shelley tried to seem cool and amused and casually charming at one and the same time, like Meryl Streep.

"Well, it's only the most wonderful thing that ever happened," she said nonchalantly. But she couldn't keep it up. She laughed with pleasure.

"You see, it's absolutely my big break," she bubbled. "I wanted to come back to Canby Hall again, and Baker House, and 407, and everything, before my career really takes off. Afterwards, I don't know how it will be. I'll probably be giving my entire life to my work, and who knows where it might take me. New York? California? Europe?" Shelley paused and wrapped her arms around her knees. "Being here like this, in dear old 407, it's hard to believe that tomorrow — "

"Is the first day of the beginning of your life," Andy said. "I think that's a terrific thought."

Shelley nodded vigorously. "So do I," she said with enthusiasm. "You'd never guess how it happened. It was unbelievable. It was only two weeks ago. Imagine. Just two weeks ago, the director of Center Stage was visiting one of my professors because they're old friends. And the director happened to mention that he still hadn't cast one of the women's parts in the new play he was doing here. Well, my professor asked him to let me try out. And he did. And I did. Was I ever nervous, but you know, well, he offered me the part."

"And you said yes," Andy said.

"You can believe it."

"Oh, boy," Andy said.

"And how." Shelley agreed. "I don't dare pinch myself. I might wake up. You see. . . ."

"I mean, she couldn't be nicer but she didn't stop. She didn't want to leave," Jane reported later to Maggie Morrison, their next-door neighbor, as she opened her geometry book. "After a while, Toby just said excuse me and took off. And I knew you were waiting."

"Well, let's get down to do this, ugh, stuff," Maggie said, squinting a little. Maggie wore her huge glasses on top of her fuzzy dark hair almost as often as she perched them on her nose. "Let's go. We've got problems here I don't even understand."

In the birch grove in the oval park in the center of Canby Hall, dorms on one side, school buildings on the other, was an old fashioned bronze statue of the school's mascot, a lioness. A plaque embedded in the stone base of the statue said it was a gift of the class of 1917, in honor of the twentieth anniversary of the founding of Canby Hall. The statue was green with age, except for its ear, which shone like gold in the late-day sun. Hardly a girl passed through Canby Hall who did not feel the need, more than once a year, to rub one ear or another. The left ear was for luck. The right ear was for passing tests.

"I used to do this every time I was in a school play," Shelley said to Andy as she carefully rubbed the left ear of the lioness. "It brought me luck then. I hope it will now, too. Of course, I've been lucky already. Some actors spend their whole lives waiting for the kind of big break I've gotten, and they never get it." She rubbed the lioness's left ear again.

"I really came back to Canby Hall just to do this. It's better than knocking on wood."

Andy felt a bond with the older girl. She felt that she understood Shelley's passion about a career as an actress in a way her roommates didn't. She had the same passion herself, for dancing.

They ambled along companionably. A few girls greeted Andy and did some staring. Shelley played a little to the audience, even once smiling and dropping a little curtsy, but Andy was puzzled. Finally she caught on and laughed.

"It's our color-coordination," she said.

Andy was wearing pale lavender tights with thick crushed-down pink socks and a sweat shirt that was a deeper lavender. Coupled with Shelley's all-orange, the effect was peacock-brilliant.

They left the birch grove and walked across the lawns toward the orchard and open meadow.

"That building over there, the arts building? That's where I discovered I wanted to be an actress," Shelley said.

"I came here wanting to be a dancer," Andy said. "I knew that's what I wanted to be when I was eight years old." And as they walked, they each told the other about their ambitions. Shelley talked about her boyfriend back in Iowa who she hoped she wasn't sacrificing by coming here to Boston, and Andy knew what she meant about sacrificing because she had missed lots of good times in order to practice.

". . . But I never really feel it's a sacrifice," Andy said, and Shelley agreed, saying she felt the same way. Andy thought Jane or somebody should definitely write an article for the Canby Hall newspaper about Shelley's big break.

"Of course, everything's not going to be one hundred percent rosy," Shelley admitted. "I have to play the piano in one scene, and I don't know how."

Andy stopped in her tracks.

"Do they know you can't play the piano?" she asked.

Shelley giggled. "Don't tell anybody," she said. "I once read in a book that an actor never should admit he can't do something. If a part calls for you to tap dance, or talk in sign language, or anything like that, when the director says can you do it, you say yes. Then when you have the part, and rehearsals begin, you quick as anything learn what you have to know."

"That's sure not the way it is with dancing," Andy said, laughing. "If you don't know how to do a *tour jeté,* you just don't know how. If you try to fake it, you can hurt yourself badly."

Afterward, she didn't know why she'd said exactly that.

CHAPTER TWO

Toby and Jane came into the dorm together, relieved that classes were over for the day. Jane dropped her things on a chair and pulled the mail from the 407 slot.

"Let's see what we have here," she said, sorting through it while Toby looked over her shoulder. "My Boston paper. Andy's letter from home. . . ." She hoisted the thick envelope for a second before returning it to the slot for Andy to pick up when she came in. "I don't think either of my parents could write me a letter this long if they were telling me the whole history of the Barretts. And Andy gets one almost every other day. It's marvelous." She shook her head. "Here's a catalogue for you, Toby. And one for me. And one for Andy. It's the same catalogue for each of us. I weep for all those wasted trees."

"Meaning?" Toby asked, but her attention

was on a pale gray envelope she saw half-hidden under the pile of junk mail in Jane's hand.

"You know what I mean. All the trees they have to cut down to make the paper for this junk," Jane explained firmly. "Forests and forests," she said more vaguely as she, too, noticed the gray envelope. She pulled it out from the rest and examined it. "I think this letter's for you, Tobe," she said.

"Yeah," Toby said, wishing she didn't feel a blush zooming up her cheeks. "I'll just take it, thanks."

"Could I possibly recognize that handwriting?" Jane said teasingly, holding the envelope out of Toby's reach. "Could that possibly be another letter from Neal?"

"I wouldn't be a bit surprised," Toby answered. "Okay, Jane. Hand it over. It's mine."

It was certainly true that Neal Worthington, also known as Cornelius Worthington III of the Boston Worthingtons, lifelong friends of the Boston Barretts, had come into Toby's life through Jane the year before. Toby and Neal were now special friends; the lanky, horse-riding, red-headed daughter of the Texas plains and the son of most proper Boston had met and meshed. During the past summer they had stayed in touch through short funny letters — Boston to Rio Verde, Rio Verde to Boston — and even though they now were back in school and within easy telephone range, they kept up the letter writing.

Toby got her envelope, grinned at Jane, sat down on the bottom step of the stairway to the second floor, and let her books slide from her lap as she opened and read through Neal's latest.

Jane, longing to know what Neal was writing to her roommate, decided the better part of discretion called for her to stay where she was, as far from Toby as possible, until the urge to be nosy went away. She dropped most of her mail — two other catalogues and an announcement that she could win a trip to Hawaii if she wanted to sell magazine subscriptions — into the wastebasket and flopped down on the nearest sofa to read her Boston newspaper. She didn't look up, not once.

"Hey, Jane, this is a gas," Toby exclaimed after a while. "Neal seems to be talking about horses. Well, about *a* horse. Isn't that strange? You know he's practically scared of horses." She reread the letter.

"Is Neal afraid of horses?" Jane seemed surprised, but Toby didn't notice.

"He says he's got a surprise for me . . . mmm . . . mysterious!" But apparently horses were all Neal was talking about. Jane saw a soft smile on Toby's face. Then Toby looked up and the smile changed to her familiar grin. "Well, seems we're going to visit a horse that will be at Randy's farm on Saturday. Neal says he'll pick me up here at noon, and I should wear boots," she said.

"When don't you wear boots?" Jane laughed.

"When I'm sleeping?" Toby asked mock-seriously.

"Right," Jane said.

Toby folded the letter, put it in its envelope, and stuck the envelope into the pocket of her jeans as Jane watched, chewing her lip.

Jane and Neal had practically grown up together and for a while had even considered themselves romantic friends. But Jane knew he never felt for her what he did for Toby, and that she never liked him in the same way Toby did. Jane thought of Beau Stockton, the cowboy she'd met and really liked the past summer when she and Andy had visited Toby's home in Rio Verde. Toby's childhood friend had turned into a romance for Jane. She wondered if the feeling between Toby and Neal was the same sort of thing. Jane noticed that another revealing blush was reddening Toby's cheeks.

"It'll be nice to see old Neal," Toby said as casually as she could.

There was a small TV in the far end of the Baker House lounge. Late every afternoon, Ms. Betts, the housekeeper, settled herself in front of it to listen to the fifteen-minute local news program. She was a Greenleaf native —

"My family was farming in Greenleaf before there ever was a Canby Hall," as she told each new class of girls — and always wanted to know the Greenleaf news. The program was repeated, with late-breaking news added, at one in the morning, "for the bakers and milkmen," as she said, but she herself could hardly be expected to stay awake that late to hear it.

As Jane relaxed on the sofa riffling through the pages of her newspaper, more girls came trooping in from classes. Among them came Andy, dashing in to change into her practice tights before dashing off again to a dance class at the Student Center. Room 407's neighbor, Dee Adams from California, who even after a day at school in New England always looked as though she had just been surfing on the biggest waves in the Pacific, dropped down next to Jane. The noise level in the lounge rose higher and higher until it was so high that it took a full minute before anybody heard Ms. Betts excited voice.

"Come and look, everybody. Our Shelley Hyde's on Pete McIver's show," she called out.

She turned the sound up and everybody did come and look, Andy especially, although she was in a rush. Even Merrie Pembroke, the tall, thin Baker House housemother whose face with its large gray eyes went surprisingly well with her customary faded old jeans and stretched-out sweat shirt. A few of the girls had made bets on the sweat shirt: some thought its original color was red, others said purple. There was no way of telling.

The girls and Merrie watched entranced. There on the small screen sat Shelley, smiling brightly but a little nervously at the interviewer, then into the camera, then again at the interviewer. Every once in a while she ran a hand through her blonde hair. She was wearing a simple pale green skirt and matching sweater with a tiny lace collar and her back was as straight as a ramrod as she sat in her chair.

"She looks like you, somehow, Jane," Dee whispered to Jane, grinning.

"Now, Shelley Hyde, I know you're not a stranger to Greenleaf . . . ," Pete McIver was saying from behind his desk. He was a young man with graying hair and a thick mustache, a friendly manner, and a deep, velvety voice. Ms. Betts adored Pete McIver.

"Yes. I mean, no. I mean. . . ." Shelley struggled to seem calm and poised. "I'm a Canby Hall alumna, Pete," she said. "That's part of the reason I'm so glad to be back in this neck of the woods." She paused. Pete McIver cleared his throat. "I mean, coming to Boston for my play meant I could visit Canby Hall. I love Greenleaf, I love Canby Hall, and it's a great pleasure being back."

"Well, we're happy to have you here. Now, I'm sure you want to tell us a little something about your play, Shelley Hyde, or" — he chuckled, — "do we have to go seek it out ourselves?"

"Hyde and go seek. . . ." Ms. Betts threw her head back and laughed with pleasure at Pete McIver's wit.

"Oh, of course I want to talk about the play. It's called *Leaving the Forest*, and it's about a man and a woman and another man, and they want to go to, well, it's hard to explain the plot. . . ."

"She's lost," Jane murmured.

"But she looks good, doesn't she?" Dee said, sounding both surprised and impressed.

Andy nodded, her eyes glued to the screen. "She really does."

"I play the part of Agnes," Shelley was saying. "It's a small part, Pete, but, may I tell you something, just between you and me?"

"Sure, Shelley Hyde, you can tell me and all my viewers, eh?"

Shelley smiled. "Well, since they're *your* viewers, Pete . . . ," she said, lowering her eyes and then raising them to his. "This is my very first professional part."

Pete McIver glanced off-camera where he clearly got a signal to hurry. "Hey, that's great. Well, from Greenleaf's Canby Hall to Boston's Center Stage, Shelley Hyde, at the start of a great career. We've been — " he said, trying to go into his closing.

"Oh, I hope so," Shelley interrupted.

"Yes, good luck and — " Pete McIver said.

"Thanks a million, Pete. I just hope everyone will come to see me . . . ," Shelley giggled.

Dee hooted, and Andy said "Shhh."

"I mean, come to see the play," Shelley hurried to explain.

"We've been visiting with Shelley Hyde, alumna of Greenleaf's Canby Hall, who will be appearing in *Leaving the Forest,* a new play being presented at Center Stage in Boston. You can see *Leaving the Forest* starting . . . what is that opening date, Shelley?"

"Two weeks from Wednesday," Shelley said. She smiled at Pete McIver and then turned and looked directly into the camera, which obligingly zoomed in on her until the whole screen was filled with Shelley's pretty face. "I just hope the girls in Room 407 at Baker House are watching. If you are, Andy and Toby and Jane, you're cordially invited to be my guests on opening night. . . ."

"Isn't that nice. Hope you're watching, girls. Well, it's so-long, Shelley Hyde, and so-long to you and you until one in the morning . . . from Pete McIver, signing off."

The program was over.

"My, wasn't that lovely!" Ms. Betts declared, smoothing down her flowered dress.

"Hey, did you hear what she said?" Andy asked the room. "Jane, you think she's really invited us to opening night?" Then she gasped. "I've got two seconds to get to dance class," and she disappeared.

"Toby, you missed Shelley Hyde on Pete McIver's show," Jane said, coming into 407 where Toby was hunched over her desk. Several crumpled sheets of notebook paper were on the floor near her wastebasket.

"Was she? That's impressive! Did she say anything interesting?"

"She's happy to be back, and it's her big break."

"*That's* interesting," Toby said.

"Now, Toby," Jane said, but she had to smile. They both had agreed after that day she came by that Shelley was very nice but a little dizzy.

"Actually, she was really okay," Jane said. "I think Pete McIver's sort of dumb, but Shelley looked great and she talked, well, just like actresses on — "

"On Johnny Carson?" Toby asked with a straight face.

"Well, almost. I'm not kidding, Tobe. She just really sparkled on that screen, and I don't think it was something she was just putting on. It was as though . . . as though the camera liked her, that's how she looked," Jane said.

Toby didn't say anything to that.

"Anyway," Jane said, saving the best for the last. "She publicly invited us to be her guests on opening night."

"Did she?" Toby took a moment to absorb that. "She used the Pete McIver show to invite us to her play?"

"Yes, she did. Do you suppose we're supposed to go on Pete McIver's show to accept?"

Jane unexpectedly discovered that she was having an attack of the giggles. The fact that Toby stayed straight-faced made her laugh even harder. Toby was impressed by the invitation, but she obviously had other things on her mind.

"Hey, Jane." She waited. "Hey, Jane, come on. Jane! I've been writing to Neal. Take a look at this."

Jane finally almost stopped laughing and almost completely caught her breath. She took the page-long note that Toby gave her.

"I can't read it," she said, and she started laughing all over again.

"Jane Barrett!"

"What is it, Toby? It looks like words but it's not words."

"Well, I thought if he's going to surprise me, I'd surprise him," Toby said. "I always was a whiz at mirror writing. Heh, heh, heh! Do you think he'll be able to figure it out?"

Jane, laughing hard again, realized that the only thing she could do was to pick up a nearby pillow and throw it at her grinning roommate.

CHAPTER THREE

Neal rang the doorbell at Baker House on Saturday promptly at noon.

Toby was, as always, so pleased to see him it made her feel funny inside. She liked the way he stood, the way he wore his jeans and the thick white Irish fisherman's sweater, the way his straight smooth hair lay against his head, the way he moved toward her as she came down the stairs and into the hallway, and the way he smiled. Toby had put on her best riding clothes for the occasion — jeans, thin blue turtleneck, big green sweater, and low cowboy boots. Her curly red hair was still wet from her shower.

"Hey," Neal said, and he kissed her. The kiss landed half on her lips and half on her chin. Toby hugged him hard. Neal's occasional awkwardness, which contrasted so much with the old society polish he usually showed, always sent a wave of tenderness through her.

"Gee, it's good to see you, Toby," Neal whispered into her hair. Then he stepped back and looked so pleased and eager that Toby laughed.

"Hey, Neal," she said.

Just then Jane emerged from the lower hall where the telephone booths were. "Oh, I'm glad I caught you both. I told Cary you were coming in from Boston, Neal, and he said why don't we double? He and the band have a gig at Jake's Joint tonight. Cary says we should come to Jake's for the show, then go out later for ribs or pasta. How about it?"

"Thanks. Sounds good to me," Neal said. "Is it okay with you, Tobe?"

"Sure," she said.

"Great," Jane said. "Meet you at Jake's, say about nine o'clock?"

Toby said, "Okay," but Neal said, "Jane, why don't we come by here around nine and take you with us to Jake's Joint?"

Something inside Toby flipped upside down. It always did when Neal acted like that — when he was so considerate and kind and made good sense, too. Toby could almost hear her great-aunt Ella saying, "October Houston, that young fella has good manners."

"There's no problem, Neal," Jane said. "Cary's picking me up on his way."

"Right," Neal said.

Toby wondered if she really saw Jane wink at Neal before she walked away, her back straight and her long blonde ponytail swaying only slightly.

"Do I have to wait till we get to Randy's to find out what's happening?" Toby asked Neal, when they got into his car. Neal was driving out to Randy's farm the long way, past Greenleaf and around.

"It's a horse, Tobe, but I want to surprise you," Neal said, putting a hand against her cheek.

"Okay. If it's a horse, it'll be a good surprise," she said.

Toby enjoyed looking out of the window. They were driving past wide fields that looked as though they were resting after the harvest, fields neatly separated from each other by low stone fences and lines of trees. They went by a few pretty, white farmhouses, all neat and tidy, with barns and sometimes bright red silos that looked cared-for. Most had fences that enclosed space where cows grazed or horses nuzzled each other. Nothing was like the open range Toby was used to back home.

"Look at that," she said, pointing out the red and orange of a maple in its blaze of New England autumn. "We just never get that kind of thing in Texas. That's been one of the things I really like up here in the North, seeing the way things change every season. Back home, our desert scrub doesn't show much difference between one season and another."

As she twisted around, looking, she noticed a pair of handsome, worn, but well-shined high black riding boots on the floor in the back of the car.

"Hey, what are those?"

"My boots," Neal answered.

"But they're riding boots?"

"Sure. My riding boots."

"You don't ride, Neal!" Toby said, surprised. She began to feel indignant. "You never told me you rode."

"Well, you know, sure I ride."

Toby didn't say anything.

"I don't ride much, Tobe. I don't love it the way you do. I don't even ride the way you do."

Toby crossed her arms and slouched down in the seat. Was that the surprise?

"You'll see when we get to Randy's."

He bent over and kissed the top of her nose and made her smile. Then, for the rest of the way, he would only talk about school and what he'd been doing lately, and he asked about her history paper that she had said she was having a tough time with and. . . .

Randy was waiting for them as they drove up and stopped near the barn.

"Did he get here all right?" Neal wanted to know right away.

"As right as can be," Randy said, opening the car door. "He's a beauty, Toby. Wait'll you see him."

As they started walking toward the barn, Toby's good spirits came back full force. Neal was still terrific, and Randy, with his blond hair blowing in the breeze, his cheeks tan from summer, and his working jeans tucked into scuffed old working boots, was a good friend and a certifiable good guy. She enjoyed the barn smell as they got closer to it. Also, she was pretty sure now of what was coming. A special horse. Maybe a young horse that needed training. Maybe something interesting, like a quarter-horse or a Morgan horse.

She was right. Randy went into the barn and in a minute, led out a big, black horse that was surely good-looking, Toby thought. But they had put an odd saddle on him. It was deep in the back, flat in front, and had just barely enough sitting space in between.

"Okay, he's a beauty but I've had my laugh. Put a real saddle on that critter, Randy," Toby said.

"Toby, that horse isn't a critter. He's a dressage horse," Neal protested.

"You mean one of those horses that side-step and cross their feet and prance and all that?"

"That's it."

She hooked her thumbs into her pockets and moved around the horse, studying him.

"If my daddy saw me near a horse like that, he'd hoot me off the ranch," she said finally.

"Get up on him, Toby. I'll tell you step-by-step exactly how to handle him," Neal said.

Toby was shocked.

"Are you joking with me, Neal? You know I can handle any horse with four legs."

"Well, this guy's a little different from a western horse, Tobe."

"Every horse is different, Neal. Just give me a leg up, and I'll show you."

"Tobe, you don't understand that — "

"Come on, Neal. If you want me to ride this horse, give me a leg up."

"Toby, listen to me."

"Later, Neal. Let me get the feel of him first."

"Toby, he won't — " Neal stopped and shook his head. "All right," he said. He helped Toby up into the odd saddle and stood back. "Did anybody ever tell you you were stubborn? You're going to be sorry, Toby."

Toby took the reins in her hand, wiggled around for a moment to get accustomed to the saddle, and cooed and spoke sweetly to the horse to ease him. Then, when she felt they were both ready, she flapped the reins against his neck, dug her heels into his flanks, said, "Okay, let's go, boy," and waited for the horse to start walking. Nothing happened. "Hey, let's go," she said again and waited. She also slapped the reins against his neck again and kicked her heels against his flanks, and again she had to wait. The horse didn't move.

"Toby, you have to — " Neal started to say

something, but Toby didn't want to hear.

"Come on, you horse," she commanded. No matter what she tried, she could not get him to budge.

"Toby," Neal pleaded.

But Toby wouldn't listen.

"Hey, fella, let's *go*," she said again, more firmly, more determined. Still there was no result. The horse twitched his ears a little and that was all.

Finally, frustrated, Toby gave up. "Thanks a lot, but no thanks. I guess my western ways frighten the poor eastern thing." And before he could stop her, she was dismounting. "Sorry, guys. Let's take off, Neal. I'm hungry for some pizza."

"Give me a break, Toby. Barnaby can practically sit up and tell you his life story if you ask him the right way. Let's start over again. Please get up and let me tell you how to ride him — or, wait a minute and I'll show you."

He started for the car, where his boots were.

"No interest, Neal," Toby said, stopping him in his tracks. "I'll just stick to Maxine, thanks, if Randy'll still let me."

"Any time, Toby. You know that," Randy murmured.

Toby felt strangely desolate. Neal, who always was so understanding, didn't seem to understand the way she felt at all.

"Listen, Toby," Neal began, coming back to her. He spoke softly, gentling her. "Dressage riding is different from regular riding, that's all. The signals to the horse are different. When you learn them, it's really great stuff. I'm positive a terrific rider like you would love it."

"I know how to ride, Neal. I don't have to learn."

"Toby, at least let me show you. . . ." But the harder Neal tried to persuade her, the more Toby resisted.

"No," she kept saying. "*Please, Neal.*" Finally Neal stopped, and to her own surprise, Toby dashed to the car and quickly closed herself in it. From behind the window, she watched Neal and Randy talk together. Then, as they separated and Neal started walking toward her, she watched carefully out of the corner of her eyes as Randy led the high-stepping big black horse back into the barn.

Jane and Cary were just coming out of the dorm when Toby and Neal pulled up.

It was an astonishment to everyone — including Jane herself — that proper Jane Barrett's favorite boy in the world was a rock musician, whose hair was long enough to be tied in a tail at the back sometimes, whose Walkman headphones were as much a part of him as the sunglasses he usually wore, and who always wore an earring. Not everyone knew he was a successful rebel against the same background as Jane.

Toby had been stubbornly quiet in the car, riding back to Baker House, listening to everything Neal said about the challenge of learning a new kind of riding and how great Barnaby was. She didn't say anything when Neal said that once she got used to riding him, even showing him at a local county horse show, she'd be putting blue ribbons up all over her room. All she could think about was that she'd never before been on a horse she couldn't get to move, not from the time she was two years old and her father first put her on a pony. But she had never seen a dressage horse before, either. Her dad and the hands sometimes joked about horses who pranced around. They always said that they weren't horses a self-respecting cowboy, or cowgirl, would ride. The only decent horse was a good common working horse, like the horses on the ranch, like her Max.

"You sporting types missed a terrific performance just now," Cary said as he and Jane approached the car.

Jane explained. "Cary tried out his new song in the lounge. The only people there were Mrs. Brett . . . and me," she said.

Cary was lead singer, guitarist, and occasional songwriter in Ambulance, Oakley Prep's best rock band.

"Bet Mrs. Brett liked that," Neal said.

"Sure she did," Cary said. "How'd you like Barnaby, Toby?"

He seemed to know all about the surprise. If he did, Jane did, too. While Cary held the door open for her, it seemed to Toby that Neal and Jane on the other side of the car were whispering together, shaking their heads, exchanging secrets. Her lips got tight. A small frown appeared. The troubled feeling grew, the foreign feeling that she didn't get much any more was starting to grow in her, the feeling that she never would be completely comfortable in this pleasant New England girls' school in this pretty Massachusetts town and that she would always be a stranger. Even with Neal, even with her roommates. . . . Toby looked at Jane and Neal, their heads still together. They were probably talking in some kind of Boston code. They certainly talked the same language, Jane and Neal. Neal was probably sorry he had ever even met her. Well, that was okay with her. She knew she never had felt about a boy the way she felt about Neal, and now he probably was through with her. Just because she didn't like that fancy horse. Well, she didn't, that's all. Dressage. Dress-*ahhge*, she drawled out dramatically to herself. What a dumb word! Who needed that?

"S'long, Neal," she said, jogging up the walk to the entrance of Baker House.

Neal, shocked, came running after her. "Hey, wait, Toby."

"Toby," Jane called, but Toby was already in the dorm.

* * *

Andy came tearing down the stairs, displaying a fan of theater tickets.

"Saw you from upstairs. Guess where I've been," she demanded gaily. Toby didn't answer.

"I met Shelley in Greenleaf for breakfast. Isn't that too much? Well, here they are, Toby. Four tickets to the opening of *Leaving the Forest* next Wednesday. Three for 407, one for Merrie Pembroke who has offered to transport us to Boston in her car."

"Swell," Toby said.

"I think Shelley came back to rub the lioness's ear for the last time. She's very high on the play and her part and the way it's going, but she said she better be on the safe side. You just missed her."

"Sorry," Toby said.

Andy caught the tone.

"Toby, is something the matter?"

"Nope," Toby said.

Andy cocked her head and observed the tight, closed look of her friend's face.

"Hey, it's me, your old pal Andy."

"I'm okay," Toby said.

Only I don't much feel like going out with Neal and Jane and Cary, she was thinking. Darn, she was being dumb. Why was she bothered so much?

"Hey, Toby, we're waiting for you," she heard Jane call from outside.

Chapter Four

Each girl felt the excitement of going to Shelley's opening night in her own way, but at three-thirty on the afternoon of the big event, the major discussion among them was whether to dress up or dress down.

"Well, I'm for dramatic and sleek at the same time. I'm wearing my skinny skirt and my most terrific loose sweater," Andy announced.

Jane decided on her pink silk dress, simple but elegant, with an evening jacket. "I'm sure that's proper, and anyway. . . ." She burrowed under the pile of things on her bed, and found the jacket. "Anyway," she said, "this is made of magic wool. Look. No creases."

"That's magic, all right," Andy agreed. She loved her roommate Jane, but she would never be able to understand that messiness bit.

Toby was being daring. She was finally wearing the gray blouse with red and blue stripes and the long gray skirt Andy had absolutely forced her to buy in Greenleaf.

"All that skirt, Andy?" Toby had protested.

"It's either that, or the mini-mini over there," Andy had answered.

"I wouldn't know how to walk around in a skirt coming down so close to my ankles."

"You would, too. If you have to, you can always practice in the room. That stripe is sensational with your red hair. She'll take it," Andy had said to the saleswoman. Then Andy had nudged her into buying really cute shoes with funny heels to go with the skirt.

Toby put on the outfit and looked at herself in the mirror. Not bad.

"I can't say I think Shelley Hyde is the greatest thing that ever walked into Room 407," she admitted. "I'd be lying if I said I did, but I do appreciate her invitation to the opening and the party afterward, and the least I can do is dress myself up for it."

Andy cheered.

"That's the spirit, Toby. It's just that you probably never met a real actress before."

That was all right with Toby, but she didn't think she'd say so out loud.

"What time did Merrie say to meet her?" Jane asked.

"Four o'clock downstairs," Toby said.

"On the dot," Andy added.

For twenty minutes after that, Room 407 whirred like a machine. When put to the challenge, the girls could get themselves dressed, fuss with their hair, put on whatever makeup they were wearing, change their minds about the eye shadow color, find the shoes they definitely wanted, decide to take jackets, then decide to take coat sweaters instead, then decide on jackets again, and still meet a deadline.

At four o'clock sharp, bubbling with anticipation, they were in the entry hall, saying good night to Maggie and Dee and a few of their other friends who had gathered to wave them off. Merrie tooted the horn of her car, and the girls dashed out.

"All set?" Merrie asked as they buckled in.

They were on their way. They would have time for a stop at McDonald's, which beat the school dining hall, and besides, they didn't want a full dinner. They'd be having supper — that's the way Shelley put it — afterward, with Shelley and the rest of the cast and all the Center Stage people.

There was an odd extra thrill for Jane in this jaunt to Boston. For the first time in her life, she was going to her hometown but not going home at all.

Toby had a little extra funny feeling, too. She was thinking of Neal. She hadn't had a letter from him since the Saturday at Randy's. Of course, she hadn't written to him, either. She half-wondered if he just might show up at this opening night performance. Not that he could. He lived in Boston but was at school in the suburbs of the city. He couldn't just take off, even if he wanted to.

There was a big poster outside the little theater.

CENTER STAGE COMPANY, INC.
presents
LEAVING THE FOREST
a new play by
MERLE GLENDENNING
directed by BARRY CASE
with

Cora Peters	Owen Westley
Susan Saxon	Lorraine Moss
Marvin Goldsmith	Shelley Hyde

Max Thomas Heather

As soon as they entered the lobby of the theater, Toby felt amazed. It was as tiny as a toy. "But it's pretty," Andy insisted when she saw Toby's expression. The walls were brick painted shiny white, with pictures of past productions up on one wall and on another, large pictures of each member of the cast of that night's play. Over in one corner, a bouquet of yellow roses on a little table added a festive touch.

Although the lobby was jammed with more

and more first nighters, the girls had no trouble making their way to the cast pictures. Even Toby caught the exhilaration of seeing somebody she knew in such a — well, in such a *mature* situation. Although it was not in the center, the star, position, the girls agreed that Shelley's picture definitely stood out. She had posed with her chin up, her eyes sparkling.

A bell tinkled, and yellow-painted double doors leading into the theater opened.

"All right, children, we're on our way," Andy said in her best upbeat way.

"I never should have worn heels," Toby moaned softly as she hurried to the double doors, wobbling slightly. She hoped that the theater itself would give her more breathing room.

Andy bit her lip as she looked around at the black walls of the tiny auditorium, the grid of lights overhead, the stark, bare set just standing there. She was still more excited about this theatrical happening than Toby and Jane, still vicariously involved in Shelley's excitement, but as they made their way inside, she had to admit to herself that she *had* expected both lobby and theater to be more impressive, more like the real theater in downtown Boston where she had seen the New York Ballet when they came on tour.

"This place used to be a firehouse," she heard the man ahead of them tell his companion.

* * *

A tall skinny boy wearing a yellow T-shirt with "Center Stage" written across it in black letters led them to their seats.

"Shelley has one of those T-shirts. She says it's for her memory chest," Andy murmured to Toby.

"How dumb," Toby said.

"Tob-*ee*," Andy hissed.

"I'm sorry. Honestly, Andy, I'm trying."

They all tried to look as casual as possible as they walked behind Merrie, who was following the usher. But Andy had to poke Toby and Toby poked Jane.

"He's *gorg*'," Andy whispered, using a Shelley-ism. Jane agreed by pointing to the usher, simply by wiggling her eyebrows.

After he showed them their seats with a wide smile, which each girl, and Merrie, too, gladly returned, he went away. They all were settling in, when Jane suddenly gasped. "I know these seats!" she exclaimed. "They're the old seats from Symphony Hall."

Andy and Toby looked where Jane was looking. What they saw were practically ancient, attached-to-each-other theater seats, with curving dark wood arms and ornate wood frames upholstered in deep red velvet that was worn so thin the wood underneath showed through.

A woman sitting nearby heard Jane and turned. "You're absolutely right," the woman said. "Look, Henry," she said to her husband.

Jane studied the back of the seat in front of her.

"They used to have plaques on them. Sure. See?" She pointed to a rectangle of lighter wood complete with four tiny nail holes. "That's where the plaque was. Wouldn't it be funny if one of these seats we're sitting in used to have a plaque with the name of my parents on it, or my grandparents, or my great-grandparents? For giving money to Symphony Hall . . . you know. . . ."

Her voice tapered off.

"I can't help it." She straightened up. "I'm never going to stop being proud of being a Boston Barrett."

Andy couldn't resist reading the program notes about Shelley out loud.

"SHELLEY HYDE (*Agnes*) makes her Boston debut with *Leaving the Forest.* She played Masha in the Denton, Iowa, Little Theater production of *The Three Sisters.* She also appeared in Denton productions of *Outward Bound* and *The Late Christopher Bean.* Hyde is a graduate of Canby Hall School in Greenleaf and attended Denton College."

Merrie studied her own playbill.

"Attended? That *is* what it says. Hmmm."

Andy read it again, to herself this time, imagining what it must be like when you finally see your first program note in a professional performance, imagining it for herself — ANDREA CORD dancing the role of Giselle. . . .

"One of these years we'll be reading that kind of thing about you, Andy," Toby said, leaning across Jane.

It was so mind-reading, and so kind, that Andy had to gulp before she could say, "Thanks, Toby."

Well, maybe the theater wasn't what she expected, Andy thought — so small, and those cast-off old seats — but as she looked around, she decided she loved being in it. It was definitely and wonderfully off-off-Broadway in Boston, and there was an air of excitement stirring the audience. It thrilled her that she would be seeing a new play with a part being acted by someone she actually knew. The lights dimmed in the theater until it went black. Then slowly the lights came up again, and the play began.

"There she is," Andy whispered to Jane, and she sat up even straighter than usual, holding her breath, as Shelley came on stage. Andy felt her heart absolutely jump. It was such an odd feeling to see someone she had walked with around the Canby Hall campus, someone she had shared confidences with — to see someone she *knew* up there, acting in a play.

Shelley was taking the part of a young woman who was supposed to be torn between going away with a young man or not going with him. Andy noticed how Shelley used body movement as well as words to show that she was troubled and undecided. She plucked at her skirt, nibbled at her fingers as though she were biting her nails, rocked back and forth on her heels. As a dancer, Andy was very aware of the importance of such movements. She glanced quickly at her roommates. Did they notice how eloquently Shelley moved? She didn't think so. Jane seemed absorbed in the play itself, and Toby had her grumpy face on.

It's funny, she thought turning her attention back to Shelley, that while acting the hesitant young woman in the play, Shelley was also still the real Shelley, running her fingers through her hair the way she always did, and when she talked, talking with the tone she always spoke with. In a moment, though, Andy found herself wiggling in her seat. Shelley or no Shelley, she couldn't altogether figure out what was happening on the stage and she definitely couldn't understand why all the conversations in the play seemed to consist more of pauses than they did words. Andy decided that while she loved watching Shelley, she didn't think she liked the play very much.

If she had been able to read Toby's mind, Andy would have discovered that Toby was having the same kind of reaction. Toby slouched in her seat, feeling almost embarrassed as she watched Shelley and the other actors walking in and out and around the scenery. The scenery was only a series of pale panels, one with an opening that was supposed to be a door and two others with cutouts that were supposed to be windows. How could those people up there not feel silly, she wondered.

Shelley was looking beseechingly at the man while an older woman who was supposed to be the young man's mother told him he must return to the city.

"Doesn't she have any lines? Isn't she going to say anything?" Jane leaned over and whispered very softly into Andy's right ear. At the exact same time Toby, on Andy's left side, whispered just as softly, "This is a dumb play." Staring straight ahead at the stage, Andy nodded. It was hard to tell who she was answering.

As the play went on, the fidgeting increased. Jane noticed that even Merrie was sliding down in her seat.

Toward the end of the play, when Shelley had the piano-playing scene she had told Andy about, the whole audience was definitely restless. The sounds of movement, rattling, even candy wrappers crinkling seemed almost as loud as the music and voices on stage. When the man in the play stopped Shelley's piano playing with a kiss, there was a murmur of laughter.

Hey, that wasn't supposed to be funny, Toby thought. Or was it? she wondered.

The girl Shelley played was finally giving up the man. She was telling him that he should leave her here where she belonged and go back to the city where his own life bloomed. It was a speech with rising and falling moods — the young woman's grief at losing her man, the sureness of her decision to send him away, her faltering resolution, her forced gaiety intended to reassure him. As Shelley made her long speech, giving up her great love, the audience quieted. There was a gathering up of attention focused on the stage. When the scene ended the audience as one person let out its breath.

"Shelley's big scene was the best thing in the whole play. Everything after was unnecessary," Jane said as they came out of the theater.

Andy nodded agreement. They had applauded all the cast heartily at the curtain calls, but when Shelley stepped forward to take a solo curtain call, Andy had stood up and clapped so hard her hands stung.

"Let's just wait here for Shelley and her friends," Merrie said, moving out of the way of the departing audience.

There was Shelley's opening night party to go to.

Chapter Five

The restaurant was just a little way down the street and around a corner from the theater, and the girls, along with all the people whose names were on the poster outside the theater, were making their way there, walking in smaller and larger groups.

Merrie had made instant friends with Lorraine Moss, who played Shelley's mother in the play and "who acts like my mother offstage too," as Shelley fondly reported. They were ambling right behind Andy and Toby and Jane. Jane thought she heard Merrie say something nice about the play.

In the first minutes after Shelley emerged from the stage door, the girls had hugged her and showered her with praise, every enthusiastic compliment they could think of, "and we're really sincere, Shelley," Jane had said a few times. She almost had added that they enjoyed her more than they did the play itself but thought better of it. Now they were content to listen as they walked alongside Shelley who was talking with some of the other members of the cast. Every once in a while, however, Shelley turned full face and full smile to them.

"You really *really* liked it, didn't you!"

"Absolutely, Shelley," Jane or Andy said. "You were marvelous."

Directly ahead of them all, the tall skinny usher, his yellow T-shirt visible under his open denim jacket and endless fringed wool scarf, was nervously checking the small portable TV he was carrying.

"They like to have an extra TV handy, for the reviews," Shelley commented with a shudder.

As they went through the dark street to the after-opening party, a big nervousness seemed to fill the chilly late-night air.

"But it's understandable," Shelley told them when Andy, without being cold, said she had the shivers. "We all have them. Until the reviews! But I'm sure it's silly to worry. The show went well. I felt it."

The restaurant where the party was held was cozy. A fire burned in a big fireplace and old prints hung on the walls. There were booths in front and back, a long table set up with a buffet of hamburgers and fried chicken and salads and sodas, and visible from almost everywhere, an enormous TV hanging from the ceiling.

As the theater people trooped in, the restaurant owner, a big bluff man, changed the channel from the sports channel to the station that did local news.

The TV determined the choice of restaurant, Shelley told the girls, passing on to them a bit of knowledge that they all knew had recently been passed on to her.

"If he weren't cooperative, we'd have to go somewhere else," she said. "We want to see the reviews the minute they're on the air."

Shelley was trying to appear as though she had gone through this opening night experience a million times, but she couldn't really carry it off. Under the thin surface of Shelley the actress was still Shelley the warm and vulnerable girl who had first come to Canby Hall five years ago. Every single member of the company knew it was her first play, her first real opening, and Lorraine Moss was not the only one who liked her and tried to look after her. With her bubbling enthusiasm, Shelley had won over the whole cast. Now, after the weeks of rehearsal that made them like one very large family, they all understood the excitement, the enthusiasm, the fear, and the relief that were tumbling together inside her. They felt it, too, but it was not new for them.

"Shelley, baby, try to take it easy and have

a good time. You've got a long wait ahead of you," said an older, slightly balding man who seemed to the girls to be the in-charge person.

"But the news will be on in only an hour, Michael," Shelley said, puzzled, frowning.

"Gonna be a very, very long hour, baby."

Shelley laughed.

"I'll try to survive, Michael. Michael Moore, have you met my friends from my old school? They loved the play. Michael's our company manager, girls. He's a very important man," Shelley said with a twinkle in her eye.

"Hi, girls," the man said with enthusiasm. "Why don't you sit down right here where you can get a good view of everybody?"

Toby had been sure she would feel awkward at this party from the moment she first heard about it, and she was, in fact, wishing she were anywhere else. But Andy and Jane were surprised at their feelings. Back at Baker House, they had been excited about the whole evening and had not expected to feel as they did at this moment, a little out of place, not sure of what to say to people. Instead of chattering away as they usually were able to do so easily, they found themselves smiling shyly and obediently sitting where Michael told them to sit. Shelley claimed a seat next to them. Except Shelley was too fidgety to sit anywhere.

"Are you comfortable? Good. Why don't you go right up and help yourself to supper —

beat the crowd," she said with a laugh. "That's right, isn't it, Michael? I want to find Lorraine and Merrie. You'll be all right, won't you . . . ? I'll be right back."

She vanished.

"So you're Shelley's friends, well . . . well." Michael leaned back in his chair, hesitated — Jane decided he didn't know what to say to girls their age any more than they knew what to say to him — but then he pointed a finger at them, one after the other.

"I'm going to tell you something. Your friend Shelley's an actress. She's a real talent. She doesn't always show it, but she's got it all — talent first, sure, but she's got the ambition, too, and the kid works hard — she didn't know anything at the beginning of rehearsals. . . ."

Andy's mind skipped to Shelley's admitting she didn't know how to play the piano even though she had told the director of the play that she could do it. Her piano playing during the performance had sounded fine, even better than that.

". . . but every time Barry" — the girls knew he meant Barry Case, the director — "knocked her down, she was up and ready to listen and learn. Yes, she's got the stuff. You remember I told you. She's got a real future in this business." He laughed. "But don't tell *her* I said so. I'm supposed to be the mean old man around here. Come on, now let's get some food."

As they walked to the buffet table, the company manager was sidetracked and the girls made their way, helped themselves, and returned to where he had seated them.

The skinny usher set up his TV on a table near theirs. When he was sure it was in the right place, plugged in and working, he plopped himself down next to them and smiled that incredible smile.

"Carlton Hunt," he announced with a pleased expression on his face.

"Hi," they said, Jane first, then Andy and Toby. Toby was nearest, so she told him their names, yelling to be heard over the increasing noise of the party.

"We're friends of Shelley Hyde," Jane told him. "From her old school. Canby Hall? In Greenleaf? I'm from Boston but the school's in Greenleaf. Do you know where that is? We're roommates in the room Shelley used to live in. With *her* roommates. Shelley came to visit the dorm last month and invited us. . . ."

Jane suddenly realized she was babbling. She was a little nervous and excited being at a theatrical party, she decided.

Toby sat silent, eating her hamburger, sipping her soda, watching and listening. She wasn't enjoying the charged-up theatrical atmosphere. Mostly she wasn't sure of the people. Underneath their flash, she decided they weren't really all that friendly. During the walk to the restaurant, one of the actors had flashed her a dazzling smile but then had turned to somebody else immediately. Toby didn't mind weird, but she also couldn't stop gaping at two members of the cast who were wearing matching black leather pants, black pullovers, long black scarves and black derbies. The truth of the matter, Toby acknowledged to herself, was that this world of Shelley's, including maybe Shelley herself, just wasn't her thing.

Shelley returned to the table, bubbling.

"Lorraine and Merrie will be here in a minute. Oh, that looks delicious. I can't wait to get to the buffet. I'm starving. Are you comfortable? Honest, now? Have you met everybody? Are you having a good time? Andy, see that man over there? Owen Westley. He was a dancer with the Cleveland ballet before he became an actor." Shelley held out her hand. "Want to meet him?"

"I'd love to," Andy said.

"It's not that she's not being as nice as anything," Toby said to Jane when Shelley floated off again, now with Andy in tow. "It's that. . . ." She threw her arm out, indicating the room of people, the atmosphere. "Sorry, I just don't go for this."

"Aren't you an actress?" Carlton asked.

Toby was so shocked she almost gasped. "Me? Heck, no."

"I don't mean now," the usher said. "I mean, aren't you going to be when you're out of school? You should be. You look like Katharine Hepburn in her old movies. I'm working my way through college right now, but the minute I get that diploma in my damp hands, it's Center Stage full time for me. *On* stage."

"No, not me. Andy wants to be a dancer, but when I get finished with all my eastern schooling," Toby said that with a smile, "I'm going back to my dad's ranch in Texas and run cattle."

"No kidding."

"And ride horses. That's what I like to do better than almost anything else."

"Really? I know about horses."

Toby immediately perked up. "Hey, do you?"

"Sure," he said. "I'm one myself. A work-horse."

Toby groaned and laughed at the same time.

"I am. Ask anybody," he insisted. "Apprentices in a theater always work harder than everybody else."

He jumped up. Someone had switched on the little TV set and was fussing with it. "Go away. Don't touch that machine. It's set for — "

"Hey, quiet everybody. Here it comes," someone yelled.

The noise abruptly hushed. The news programs were beginning. The Baker House girls found themselves huddling together, wanting to stay out of the way, to watch but not intrude. There was a low murmur of conversation as Shelley, Lorraine Moss, and almost everybody else in the restaurant edged closer to the big television screen.

An earnest man on the big screen started giving the weather report.

"Enough," shouted someone.

They had to wait, itching with impatience, through the weather report, international news, local news — which went on and on about a Boston woman who had quintuplets — until finally Jim Cricket, the entertainment reviewer, was on the air. The Canby Hall girls could hear the mass intake of breath as he began to talk:

"Nobody could wish success more than I do to Center Stage, the brave company led by Barry Case and Michael Moore, which is dedicated to bringing new works by new playwrights to Boston," he began. "But good wishes do not a good play make. This evening Center Stage presented the first production of their second season. It is *Leaving The Forest* by Merle Glendenning, a comedy — or it might have been meant as a tragedy. I couldn't tell."

The quiet of the listeners changed quality. It suddenly became leaden.

"I wish I could find one good thing to say about this production," the reviewer went on. "The set, a clever assortment of panels and doorways frequently moved to represent different rooms as well as a forest, seemed to have as much trouble deciding what was going on as the actors did. I don't know who this show was supposed to appeal to. Certainly not me and, to judge by their reactions, not the audience either. . . ."

Shelley dropped her head into her hands.

There was a dreadful silence in the restaurant as the reviewer's voice went on with his devastating comments, a silence finally broken when Lorraine Moss abruptly reached up and switched off the set. In the hollow moment that followed, Jane, Toby, and Andy moved closer to each other and, as one, looked over at Shelley.

"Now wait a minute," somebody shouted. "That's only one guy. How about Pete McIver?"

But the group huddled around the small TV who had already heard McIver shook their heads and turned off the set.

"No good," one of the actresses said, turning into the arms of one of the men for consolation. "Jones at least mentioned you, Shelley," she said over the man's shoulder. Shelley looked up hopefully, but the actress simply shook her head.

Merrie quickly went to Shelley, and the girls, too, clustered around. Shelley looked devastated. She had turned ghostly pale, as though shock had drawn a white line around her lips, wiped away all the pink from her cheeks. Only her eyes had not faded. Instead, they darkened, going from their usual sunny blue to what seemed blue-black.

"But — " She struggled to speak, to understand — "But . . . didn't we all think it was good?"

Surprisingly, Toby was the first of the girls to find something to say. "You were terrific, Shelley, no matter what those dumb reviewers said."

"Toby's right," Andy quickly added. "You were great. You thrilled me."

Shelley listened to the girls, but then she shook her head.

"If we were so great, why did they say those terrible things?" she asked.

"They don't know anything," Again, surprisingly, it was Toby who spoke up.

"Please don't say anything more," Shelley said, now sitting absolutely still.

"We have to, Shelley," Jane said, putting her arm around the still figure. "Because it's true. You were wonderful."

Shelley did not respond and the girls looked at each other again. They turned to Merrie for guidance. But before anybody else said anything, Michael Moore got up from the table.

"Get the closing notice ready," he said, buttoning his jacket.

When she heard that, Shelley lifted her head

and stared straight ahead but did not seem to see anybody.

Lorraine Moss, looking paler than she had earlier in the evening, signaled to Merrie.

"I think Shelley might feel better if you left now. She'll be okay when she gets over the shock. We all will."

"You really think so, Lorraine?" Merrie asked. "I trust your judgment."

"In about five minutes, there's going to be a wake here. Just for the family, if you know what I mean. We'll be supporting each other."

"All right. Get your coats, girls, we're going now. Lorraine, I'm so terribly sorry."

"Yep, thanks. I am, too," the older actress said ruefully. "But it happens."

"Girls?" Merrie said, putting on her coat.

Andy put out her hand and touched Shelley's. "I wish you wouldn't feel so terrible, Shelley, because you really *were* wonderful." Jane came next, hugging Shelley and murmuring soothing sounds, and Toby managed an awkward little wave and smile. Then, on a signal from Merrie, they made farewells to the other people nearby and left. Merrie stayed back for a moment, putting her arm around Shelley and talking softly to her.

"It's not as though the whole world came to an end," Toby said when they got outside. "Shucks, just look up at that big starry black sky."

"Shucks yourself," Andy said. "Poor Shelley."

"Yes, poor Shelley, but" — Jane lowered her voice and the three heads moved closer together — "The play *was* awful, wasn't it?"

"I didn't understand half of it," Toby admitted. Then the heavy, unfamiliar tension of the evening exploded in her. "It was terrible, every bit of it."

Andy was suddenly furious. "Stop that. Stop it," she shouted.

"What's the matter, Andy?" Toby demanded.

"Just stop, please," Andy said quietly. "You know that could happen to me someday."

"Michael Moore said they should get the closing notices ready," Jane recalled.

They were silent after that and when Merrie Pembroke came out of the restaurant, she ushered three sad and weary girls into her car for the ride back to Canby Hall.

CHAPTER SIX

When they got back, everybody wanted to hear about the big night, but after a few days, life at Canby Hall, at Baker, and in Room 407 settled into normal.

On an early Saturday morning Toby and Andy split the last of a leftover pizza and, leaving Jane still huddled happily in sleep, went off into the day. Andy was going across campus to the arts building, where she and two other serious dancing friends had arranged to use the studio to practice some new steps before ADC, their advanced dance class, began. Toby was going to Randy's farm. They parted outside the dorm and Toby smiled as Andy turned to send her a quick wave of the hand. It must be terrific, Toby thought, to feel as *positive* as Andy did — about her dancing, about school, about everything. Toby herself was full of the grumps, and knew why, and wasn't feeling positive at all. Well, a good long gallop on Maxine would take care of any creaking she had inside herself.

"That horse still here?" she asked as soon as she arrived at Randy's. She didn't have to tell him which one she meant.

"Yes, he is."

Was Randy acting kind of cold to her? Toby hated that.

"Listen, Randy, a couple of weeks ago, honestly, I couldn't help the way I jumped off him. I was so surprised . . . I didn't mean to. . . ."

Randy smiled and handed her a steaming mug of coffee.

"Maybe you were just scared."

"How could I be scared of a *horse*?" Toby protested.

"Well. . . ."

They ambled together into the barn, both holding their mugs between their hands for warmth. On the way to Maxine's stall, they passed the stall where the big, beautiful Barnaby stood amiably looking out.

"A real warm-tempered horse," Randy remarked as they paused to look at him.

Toby admitted she didn't know what he meant.

"Oh, not hot-blooded and temperamental, like thoroughbreds. Thoroughbred racehorses are so edgy every nerve under their skin quivers. But not this fellow."

The horse came toward them and poked his head at them over the gate of his stall.

"He's not stubborn either — unlike some people I know," Randy went on.

"Come on, now, Randy. Be fair."

Randy snorted.

"Look who's talking about what," he said.

Toby covered her confusion by patting Barnaby's nose and, as somebody who had looked at a lot of horses in her time, she noticed how different he was from Max at home, even different from Maxine who right this minute was being saddled for Toby to ride.

"He's awfully heavy in his hind quarters, isn't he?" she said.

"Yeah. Stronger in the back than in the front. I haven't been around dressage horses much myself, but Neal was telling me — "

"When did you talk to Neal?" Toby interrupted.

"That day when you went off sulking in the car, Toby."

"Ouch," Toby said.

"Anyway," Randy continued, "according to Neal, the hind quarters are the engine in these fellows. That's why they can dance around with their front legs up."

"Hmph," Toby said. "Old Max is like a wheelbarrow. All his power's in front."

"That's the way it is with all the horses I've ever had," Randy said.

"But I love Max," Toby said, raising her chin into the air.

"Of course."

A stable hand went by leading Maxine out of the barn.

"I love Maxine, too," Toby added with a grin.

She patted Barnaby's nose before she went walking after Maxine and kept looking back at him as she left the barn.

Randy held Maxine's head as Toby mounted.

"Have a good ride," he said, giving Maxine a pat on the rump.

"Thanks, Randy. I mean, really, thanks for being such a good friend."

You're getting soppy, she told herself as she rode off toward the open fields. She already felt better than when she came. She always did when she rode out on Maxine, who always made her think happily of her own Max and the wide ranges where she rode in Texas.

The three roommates came to the dining hall from their assorted morning activities. Jane's activity had been mostly staying in bed reading her history assignment. She was resolved not to have to do hurry-up homework on Sundays any more. She would do it, at a leisurely pace, on Saturday mornings instead, and bed on a chilly morning had seemed the perfect place to start. She felt thoroughly virtuous as she finally tossed the book on top of the clutter on the floor around her bed and got up and showered and dressed and went out to join Andy and Toby.

"I'm for a minor shopping binge in Greenleaf this afternoon," she announced over her salad soaked in creamy Italian dressing. "Anybody want to come?"

"I might. I could use a new pair of jeans," Toby said.

"Me, I want to," Andy said, with a twinkle in her eye. "Have you ever heard of this movie *White Nights*?"

"No-o-o," Toby and Jane answered in unison.

"Okay, okay. But I may just get a video of it. And ask Merrie to let me play it on her VCR. I know I'd be tossed out of the lounge if I played it there."

"Right," Toby said.

"We ought to check with Merrie," Jane said. "Didn't she ask us to let her know the next time we go video shopping? I think there's a particular movie she wants to get."

"What movie?"

"I think it's one of those old Laurence Olivier Shakespeare things, but I'm not sure."

"Shakespeare! Ugh, how wonderful," Toby said, digging into her bowl of chocolate bread pudding.

"Well, let's go, then. To the dorm and

away," Andy said, hoisting her dance bag and standing up.

"We can't," Jane said, watching Toby actually enjoying what Jane considered the world's worst dessert. "Toby is still eating."

The girls decided to leave Toby to luxuriate in her dessert. They went back to the dorm and upstairs to Merrie's apartment to see if she wanted them to get her a video.

In the days of Alison, Baker House's former housemother, the housemother's apartment had been a great mix of color, neon, hassocks, and health-food cookies. But when Merrie moved in, she had decorated it classically New England. Sometimes, when the rainbows in Toby's corner of 407 and Andy's earth tones and art work seemed to clash *too* interestingly with her own New England corner of pale blue and old quilts, Jane went to Merrie's apartment for a cup of tea and empathy, as Merrie once laughingly described it. The room always made her feel at home, as Merrie herself did. Yes, for Jane, knocking on Merrie's door was a familiar gesture. But now, just as she began to knock, both girls heard such convulsive sobbing from inside the apartment that her hand froze. Was Merrie in her living room crying her heart out? Jane dropped her hand as though it were on fire.

"Hey, something heavy's going on in there," Andy said in a soft whisper.

"And how," Jane answered just as softly. "I wonder what it can be."

In an instant they both knew. Between the heartbreaking gulps and sobs came the sound of a familiar voice.

"Oh, Merrie, I'm such a failure . . . my life's ruined . . . what will I . . don't know what to do . . . where to . . ."

"It's Shelley," Andy gasped.

The girls knew they ought to leave. Wordlessly, with eyes only, they told each other they should not stay eavesdropping — and wordlessly, they stayed listening anyhow.

"Poor Shelley." Andy was almost crying herself.

"I left college, Merrie. Did you know that . . . I mean, my parents got my tuition back, I mean I really left. Oh, I had such a . . . such a quarrel with my family about it . . . and they finally gave in because I was going to be . . . and Paul . . . my boyfriend he'll never ever speak to me again . . . I was so . . . couldn't go back to college anyway . . . face Professor Benjamin . . . he was so sure I'd . . . oh, Merrie, such a failure . . . how can I . . . what shall I . . ."

They could hear Merrie making little comforting sounds as Shelley poured out her grief nonstop. Slowly, silently, the girls backed away from the door and tiptoed to the stairs. Then they ran down to where Toby was waiting.

Before they got out of earshot, though, they heard Merrie saying something.

"But what was she saying? Did you catch it?" Andy asked Jane as the three roommates settled next to each other in the back of the bus for Greenleaf.

"Something about the princess's room. Does that make sense?"

"Yeah. I think she must have told Shelley she could stay at Baker House for a while, in the guest room we fixed up when Princess Allegra visited."

Toby groaned.

"Toby, you're getting awful these days. I think you should stop," Jane said indignantly.

"What did I do?"

"Just now? About Shelley? Groan, groan, that's what you did. Didn't you think we could hear you?"

"Well . . . " Toby tried to think of something reasonable to answer Jane but she couldn't. "I can't help it if I just don't especially take to Shelley. Forgive me, Andy, I just don't. Everybody doesn't have to like every single person, do they . . . uh, does she . . . uh . . . oh, you know what I'm trying to say."

"Well, do you know what *I'm* saying? What's with you in general?" Jane demanded.

Toby was taken aback. "What are you talking about, Jane?" she asked.

"I'm talking about my old friend Neal."

"Neal?"

"Yes, that terrific boy you're supposed to like so much."

"What about Neal?" Toby asked, but she was beginning to feel a little uncomfortable.

"You hurt him very badly, for no good reason. I know all about what happened a couple of weeks ago with you and Neal and that horse. He was planning this terrific surprise for you, and you didn't even let him. . . ."

Toby turned to Andy for support, but Andy had tuned out. She was staring bleakly out of the window, thinking unhappy thoughts about Shelley.

Toby turned back to Jane. "Okay. You're right. It was a surprise. A horse that couldn't even move. What was the point of that?"

"Barnaby can move just as well as any horse you ever rode, Toby Houston," Jane said.

Toby hesitated. "Jane, why're you being so mean?"

"Because you don't have a clue as to what this horse business is all about, and you don't want to, and Neal — "

Toby looked so hurt and confused that Jane's anger suddenly vanished.

"Look," she said, taking Toby's hand in hers. "Barnaby belongs to Neal's aunt, the horsy one, down in Florida. She sent Barnaby up north early to get him used to, oh, the weather and all that because she wants him to be ready to show at the autumn county horse show. She wanted to board him in Boston so Neal could exercise him until she gets here. She's coming up in a month or so, I think Neal said."

"But Randy's farm isn't in Boston, Jane."

"She's nice but sometimes she doesn't catch on to things," Jane said to Andy, who smiled a little and went back to looking out of the window. "Item one: Neal told his aunt that he thought Randy would care for her precious Barnaby better than the place in Boston would."

"He was probably right," Toby said in a small voice.

"Item two: he thought it would be terrific if you let him teach you some dressage riding and *you* exercised Barnaby. He was sure you'd love it"

Toby slouched further down in her seat. "I did everything I knew, and I couldn't get that horse to budge. That never happened to me in my whole life."

"Barnaby's trained to other signals, Toby. Don't be so dense!"

There was a long, long silence. Finally Toby spoke.

"I think I owe Neal a letter," she said.

"Maybe you do," Jane agreed.

Andy turned back to her friends.

"Listen, kids, and you especially, Toby. It's going to be Be Kind to Shelley season, if we ever have the chance. I just want you to know."

The bus stopped right in front of the ice cream place and they got off.

"Meanwhile," Andy continued, "it doesn't make a bit of difference that we had lunch a half hour ago, agreed? It's time for an early afternoon banana split."

When they came back to the dorm and were approaching Merrie's room on the fifth floor, laden with videos and other packages, they practically bumped into Merrie and Shelley walking along the hallway.

"Hello, girls," Merrie said. For a flash of a second, she reminded Toby of Alison. Merrie was radiating a kindness and a warmth that Toby always had connected with Alison.

"We rented you a Laurence Olivier video, Merrie," she said. "Shakespeare. *Henry V.*"

"Did you? Thanks. That's great. Want to come see it?"

She laughed to see the battle between courtesy and an intense desire to say no playing out on the three faces before her.

"Never mind," she said. She put her arm around Shelley. "Shelley and I will enjoy it a lot, won't we, Shelley?"

Shelley smiled weakly.

"Shelley's going to be our guest for a while, on this floor. I'm showing her the guest room.

You know Shelley, a real princess once slept in that room."

Shelley smiled weakly again. When Toby saw the tear-stained, forlorn expression on the older girl's face, she felt an enormous, completely unexpected compassion. Even more, she experienced a stab of conscience so strong it almost physically hurt as she realized how right Jane was, how all-around lacking in sympathy she, Toby, had been.

"You're welcome here, Shelley," Toby said. "Anything we can do for you, any time you want company, you just whistle. And you know 407's still your room."

Jane turned and stared for a moment at Toby and then hurried to agree with her.

"Absolutely, Shelley," she said.

Shelley turned away from them all and went into the room with Merrie and closed the door.

Chapter Seven

The meeting was called in 407 on Sunday morning. In some ways, it was a protest meeting. Dee Adams, Maggie Morrison, Penny Vanderark, and a selected few others who were involved in the school's arts programs and clubs protested because they were fairly sure they were going to be asked to do something they probably did not want to do. The meeting was Andy's idea, and when Andy got onto something, as almost everyone at Baker knew, she didn't let go.

"You may have wondered why we've called you here this evening," Andy began.

"I can't do it. I don't have time. I have too much homework."

"Thank *you*, Dee. It's always nice to be able to depend on you through thick and thin and so on and so on," Andy said. "Will somebody please sit on our friend from southern California?"

After the horseplay, Andy went on.

"Okay. This is why there's a meeting. We all know that Shelley Hyde is staying here, in the guest room."

"Shelley *Hyde* is right," Penny said. "That's what she does. A lot of kids want to meet her. I do. But it's like, you can't find her. Doesn't she ever open the door to that room?"

"Not too often, not even for us," Andy said. "Every time we ask her over here — 407 used to be her room, you know — she makes excuses."

"I think she even takes her showers after lights out, so she won't have to meet anybody," Jane said, shaking her head.

"That's nuts," Maggie said.

"Sure it is," Andy agreed. "*That*'s why we're having this meeting. Shelley's really a very nice person. I mean, she's really warm and kind . . . she's nice. But right now, she's one very *unhappy* nice person. We think Baker should try to do something to cheer her up."

"I go along," Maggie said. "I'm sort of related to her anyway, you know. My sister Dana was one of her roommates here a couple of years ago."

"Part of 407's glorious history. Now, about our idea." Andy gestured to Jane to take over, and Jane unhooked her arms from around her knees.

"Well, the whole thing is that Maple Syrup

Day's coming soon," Jane said. "We thought, why don't we make a big number of it — go out and collect the buckets, of course — "

"Ah, the fine old Canby Hall tradition." Toby smiled, and the others laughed.

Maple syruping was an old Canby Hall tradition, one of many. It was corny, but fun. Early each autumn the school groundskeepers tapped the maple trees in the orchard, and later, on a day set aside as a holiday, the girls collected the filled buckets and helped cook the thin sap into thick maple syrup in large copper vats set outdoors over log fires. If there was snow on the ground, they tossed spoonfuls of the hot syrup onto the snow, which froze the syrup instantly into delicious chewy candy.

" — and later have a buggy ride and a terrific picnic . . ." Jane continued and nodded toward Andy, ". . . and make a whole big extra celebration with Shelley as the guest of honor."

"I changed my mind. I can do it. I have time. I don't have too much homework," Dee announced, "but . . . oh, can't you think of a way to make it a beach picnic?"

The girls laughed. They knew that Dee's heart belonged to surfing and swimming and sunning on Pacific beaches.

"All right. We have Dee. How about the rest of you?" Andy asked.

"I say sure," Maggie answered, and the others also agreed.

"Great. Now let's organize," Andy said.

"Well, we'll have to get picnic stuff," Jane said.

"Let's see what comes in from my family this weekend," Andy said with a shrug and a smile. Sometimes Andy was almost overwhelmed by the quantity of her parents' CARE packages. But she knew the packages were as full of love as they were of food. Fuller. "But we'll need some things from Greenleaf, too," she added.

"I'll volunteer for that," Maggie said. "What will we need? Sodas and things? I can go on the weekend."

"I'll go with you, Maggie," Andy said. "We can make a list before we go."

"Right." They pointed fingers at each other.

"I'm sure Randy will lend us a horse and his big buggy. I'll call him," Toby said.

"I don't think there's much else, is there," Jane said, "except inviting Shelley."

"Why don't *I* do that? I'll draw a funny, formal invitation that we can all sign, if you'd like," said Penny.

"There'll be some expense, but not much. We can chip in equally," Jane said.

"Don't forget that we have to have warm blankets," Toby said firmly.

She was already feeling the autumn chill in the air, and shivering at the idea of the oncoming winter. Toby had only experienced the snow and biting winds of a northeastern winter once, last year, her first year at Canby Hall, after a lifetime of south Texas winters.

"I think that's everything," Jane said.

"You must have spent the whole of English doing this," Andy said to Penny, who showed her the invitation to Shelley, finished except for color, as they walked from English class to history class the day after the meeting. "Every time I looked up from *Hamlet*, there you were, sketching away."

"Sure. Ms. MacPherson didn't notice. Anyway, doing this was much more fun than mentally redressing her, which is what I usually do in English."

"Penny!" Andy stopped abruptly in the middle of the hall and stared at her classmate. "Ms. MacPherson? Whose favorite color is navy blue? In . . . what?"

"Hip fashion, of course," Penny said mildly. "About the card. Do you like it?"

Andy burst out laughing. "I love it," she said.

The card was colored and signed by all of the girls by late afternoon. Early evening, before they went to dining hall, Andy, with Jane and Toby beside her, slipped it under Shelley's door, and the girls shared happy smiles.

"I feel really good about this," Jane said as they buttoned up their jackets and went down the stairs.

"Me, too," Andy said. "Maple Syrup Day is always goofy, anyway, and with our 'extra added attractions,' Shelley will *have* to enjoy herself."

"Hey, hold it, wait for me for a minute, will you?" Toby said, darting into the ground floor phone booth. "I want to see a man about a horse."

In practically no time, she was back after making a call.

"Randy says fine. He's got a couple of buggies, and we should come and choose."

"*You* choose."

"Saturday," Toby answered.

On the way back to Baker after dinner, the girls felt altogether good. They had been able to translate their sympathy for Shelley into something that, although it was planned to lift Shelley's spirits, lifted theirs as well.

Back in their room, the good feeling lingered on. Toby flopped on her bed, took a deep breath, and decided she finally had the strength of spirit to take out the small, flat package that Neal had sent in answer to her letter. After putting the Bangles album on the stereo, Andy and Jane settled into one of their pleasant, useless occupations. They were playing killer checkers. Even the night outside the windows seemed cozy and friendly.

A tap on the door.

Andy got up and opened it.

"Hey, Shelley."

Shelley's "Hi" was hard to hear. She was wearing the same wrap-around red robe she had been wearing when the girls had gone to see her backstage after the opening, and fluffy silver scuffs — no matter how sad she was feeling, the old Shelley showed up in those deliciously frivolous slippers.

But that Shelley *was* feeling sad was clear to them, as Andy stepped aside and Jane and Toby came forward with pleased smiles to show her how glad they were to see her. There were faint smudges of makeup on her dressing gown, but none at all on Shelley's face. Her face was wan, with red-rimmed eyes and pale, dry lips — and Andy wanted to put her arms around her and rock her gently to and fro.

"Come on in, Shelley."

"No thanks," she said, standing in the doorway. Down the hall, Maggie and Dee poked their heads out of their room, and girls on their way to the shower room stopped to look over their shoulders at the little group in the doorway of 407.

"No, I won't come in, thanks. I'm terrible company, so there's no point in inflicting myself on you. I'm here because of . . . this."

She held Penny's pretty invitation, with all their signatures, between her thumb and first fingers, as though it were something contagious.

"I can't imagine how you thought I could possibly accept this."

"Why not?" Toby asked, the edges of her sympathy for Shelley fraying slightly.

Shelley barked a little laugh.

"I just couldn't. For one thing, Merrie may be letting me stay here for a little while but that doesn't turn me into a Canby Hall girl again. Maple Syrup Day is for Canby Hall children, not grown-ups like me." Her lower lip trembled. "Not for hopeless, failed grown-ups like me."

"Oh, Shelley, no," Andy said softly. "We asked Merrie. She's coming, too. And we planned the picnic and buggy ride after the syruping for you *because* we know you're feeling rotten. We want to help make you feel better, Shelley."

Shelley was silent.

Then, "Impossible. Anyway, I can't be good company," she said. "I'm too upset about myself."

"Shelley, please don't talk like that. You're *always* good company."

"I said no. I guess you meant well but don't you understand? I don't want to do anything."

Now it was the girls who stood silently.

Shelley pushed the invitation into Andy's reluctant hand. As she did, she glanced beyond Andy and saw, on the nearest desk, the Playbills from Center Stage that she had signed: "To the Girls in Room 407, with love from Shelley Hyde — on the occasion of her debut in the professional theater!"

"Don't tell me you're keeping those things," Shelley said angrily.

"Of course we are," Jane said. "We cherish them. People are going to line up for a look at that inscription when you're a famous actress."

"Ha! A famous actress." Shelley's laugh was rough. "I saved one of them, too. I framed it and drew a thick black line around it."

"Ah, Shelley," Andy said sympathetically.

"In other words, please do me a favor. Leave me alone."

With that, Shelley rushed away to her room. She left behind three stunned roommates. Dee and Maggie, as dismayed as Andy and Toby and Jane, came into 407 to commiserate. The others who had been in on the party, responding to an instant grapevine, quickly showed up to share the disappointment and annoyance. Penny Vanderark was the only one who didn't seem upset. She simply coolly shrugged Shelley away.

"She may think she's grown-up," Penny said, "but I think she's a baby."

To everyone's surprise, Andy turned on Penny furiously.

"She's not a baby. She's just been hurt something terrible, and she's not handling it very well," Andy shouted and burst into tears.

Chapter Eight

"I don't care. She didn't have to be rude," Toby said to Jane the next morning as they walked across campus to the science building.

"I agree with you, Toby."

"I say, if she wants to be let alone, let's leave her alone," Toby continued.

"I agree completely," Jane said.

"I'm not going to do anything else to try to cheer her up. No, ma'am."

"Me, neither," Jane said. "I don't see any point in even thinking about her any more."

"Neither do I," Toby said.

Jane scuffed at the autumn leaves under her feet. "But poor Andy," she said finally. "She feels terrible."

Toby agreed with that, too. The girls who had gathered in 407 the night before had spent lots of time trying to understand Shelley's behavior, but at Lights Out they had gone back to their rooms without reaching any conclusion. Only Andy persisted in all-out compassion.

"Being rude isn't at all like Shelley, so think how unhappy she must be," Andy had insisted.

Toby and Jane split at the entrance to the building, Toby to Computer Science and Jane to dreaded Geometry where Maggie was already at her desk in the back of the room waving hello to her. Jane sat down at her desk, resolutely opened her textbook and notebook, and looked with what seemed like full concentration at Mr. Carruthers. What she really was doing was putting her mind to the Shelley problem, exactly what she agreed with Toby not to do.

Jane was surprised that she felt obliged to try to help Shelley feel happier. Shelley was saying that her life was over, but it wasn't; it couldn't be. Mr. Moore, the company manager, had said Shelley had a terrific future. Jane somehow could not watch Shelley throw that future away, as she seemed to be doing. Anybody looking at Jane just then would have seen her pause in thought, shake her head, pause in thought again, shake her head again. Finally, whoever was watching would see her relax. Jane came to what she thought was a brilliant solution — about Shelley — a second before Mr. Carruthers called her to the blackboard to solve problem four on page eighty-two. Fortunately, she managed that solution, too.

When class was over, Jane hurried to the main floor phone booths and searched around in the bottom of her handbag until she found the right change for a call to Boston.

"Mother? It's me. No, I'm fine, really. No, nothing's wrong. Mother, is anything important going on at home Saturday or Sunday? Who? Oh, that's all right. No, it wouldn't make any difference. You see, I'd like to invite a friend — well, an acquaintance — to come for the weekend. May I? It's the actress who used to have my room at Baker House, remember? Shelley Hyde, the one in the Center Stage play. What? Oh, didn't I tell you? Oh, mother, it was awful. I mean" — Jane giggled. She couldn't help herself — "Shelley was good, but the play! It opened and it *closed.*" Then Jane was earnest again, "And Shelley can't get over it." The phone box clanged. "Mother? Are you still there? That's my change and I don't have any more. May I bring Shelley next weekend? Thanks, and mother . . ." she said but they had been disconnected.

Certain that Shelley would feel restored and ready to face the world again after a weekend in the ease and tranquility of the beautiful Barrett house on Louisburg Square, Jane left the science building and went to the student lounge. She decided to give herself the treat of watching junk television for an hour during her free study hour second period.

Toby left her Computer Science class, which she had enjoyed. She hadn't even thought about Shelley. Not once. She had cleared Shelley right out of her mind. Instead, she had finished a computer project she had struggled over for weeks. She had worked out a program for her dad to use on the ranch. It had to do with weight of beef, and proportion of fat, and other things that mattered to cattle ranchers. She had finally got it exactly as she wanted it and printed it out and placed the printout safely into her notebook. Later, she would send it off to her dad as a present.

Toby didn't realize that while the front of her head was definitely not thinking about Shelley, the back of her head had been thinking about Shelley a lot. She had meant every word she said to Jane, but somehow, when she got to the main floor of the building with the present for her dad in her notebook, she found herself heading for a phone booth and ringing a familiar number.

"Hello, Mrs. Crowell? May I speak to Randy, please. It's . . . Oh!" Toby laughed. "I can never make anonymous phone calls. Everybody always recognizes my voice. . . . Randy? Hi. Your mom recognized my voice. I told her everbody does. Oh, well. Look, Randy, remember we were going to do a big bit for Shelley Hyde on Maple Syrup Day . . . yes, with your big buggy. Well, you know Shelley didn't like the idea too much so we canceled. I think she got thrown a little by so many of us trying to cheer her up at one time.

"But I have a hunch she'd feel differently if it wasn't such a mob. I bet if I took her out for a spin in your smaller buggy, the two-seater, out through some of those pretty woods past your farm . . . well, I think it'd take some of the lumps right out of her, don't you?"

Toby made a small embarrassed sound. "I know. But even if I don't like her as much as Andy does, well, I know if I were Shelley it would make me feel good, just clopping along quiet in the woods. I wouldn't say a word to her. I'd just drive the buggy. What do you think, Randy? You do? You really do? Great. Saturday? Saturday. Thanks, Randy. Um, Randy . . . Oh, never mind. So long."

No need to say anything about Neal's aunt's horse. Toby looked at her watch. She was late! She raced up the stairs to second-period Algebra.

Across the campus in the arts building, Andy's second-period class was Intermediate Ballet. It came between first-period English and third-period math twice a week, a schedule that her adviser had said at the beginning of the term was surrealistic. Andy knew exactly what she meant.

"I heard what happened to your good works project," the girl in front of her said as Andy took her place at the barre in the dance studio.

Andy did a few knee bends. "I still think . . ." she said between breaths, ". . . maybe we just . . . went about it . . . wrong. It might be better . . . if I approach her . . . by myself."

"You're a glutton for punishment," the girl said, laughing.

Andy laughed, too. "Don't you know it," she said as she bent and stretched and panted. But Andy had felt from the beginning that she could not let Shelley be alone in her misery. She had to help.

When Toby and Jane got back to 407 after classes were done for the day, each with lots of homework and a plan to help Shelley, they found Andy examining her food supplies with particular attention. Usually at that hour, it was, on Andy's invitation, dig in and find whatever was there to fend off late afternoon hunger pangs. This was different.

"What are you doing, Andy?" Toby asked.

Andy sat back on her heels.

"I'm fixing a CARE package to take to Shelley," she said. "She's a good eater, you know, and, see, this week my parents sent those chocolate doughnuts she likes."

"Shall we come with you?" Jane asked.

"No, I don't think so, if you don't mind," Andy answered. "I think I can reach her better if I go alone."

"You probably can," Toby said.

"I thought I'd take the goodies to her, and we'd have a kind of dinner together, easy-like, and talk. Maybe I can even get her out to take a walk."

Andy finished her picking and choosing and put the selected things in a box. She went to her bureau and found a red scarf and tied it around the waist of her jeans. "Red's cheerful," she told her roommates and picked up from her bed a sprig of pretty pink flowers she had put together. She tucked the flowers between a package of cream cheese and a jar of peanut butter at the top of the box and took a deep breath.

"Good luck," Jane said.

"Yeah," Toby said.

"Yeah," Andy said, too. "See you later," she added and went out the door.

The princess's room was down the hall and around the corner. To Andy, it actually seemed to send out dark rays as she stopped in front of it and tapped twice.

"Shelley? Shelley?" she softly called. "It's Andy. May I come in?" She waited for an answer but it didn't come. She tapped again. "Shelley, it's Andy."

"I don't really want to see anybody, Andy," Shelley's voice said from the other side of the door.

"But Shelley, it's me. I bring you best regards from the lioness . . . she says if she slipped this time, she's sorry but not to worry. It's going to be good luck from now on." She waited. "Shelley?"

"Not funny, Andy."

"Oh, Shelley, please. I understand how you feel."

"No, you don't."

Tears welled up in Andy's eyes. She could sense the older girl's desolation, and it made her sad.

"Come on, Shelley. You're not alone. Let me in. I've got a box of goodies and it's getting heavy."

"You don't understand, Andy."

"*Please* let me in, Shelley, and we can talk about it."

Shelley opened the door. Andy was glad to see that she was dressed. Shelley was wearing bright green sweats and the fluffy slippers.

Andy came in, juggling the box, and as she set it down, filled the room with chatter.

"Hey. I brought you the best of my parents' latest food package. Did you know that my family has a restaurant in Chicago? That's where all this comes from. We're working on a way to ship ribs."

Shelley didn't answer, but Andy didn't stop

trying. She took the sprig of flowers off the package of cheese crackers and, with a flourish, presented them to Shelley.

"For you," she said.

Shelley took the sprig and looked at it for a moment, then twirled it in her fingers and put it down.

"A funeral bouquet. Thanks. I guess that's appropriate. Look, Andy, this is very sweet of you, but you shouldn't have bothered."

"But, Shelley . . ."

"There just isn't any point to . . . oh, look, Andy, I really don't care to talk about it. I'm the greatest failure in the whole world and I know it and that's all there is to it."

"You're not!"

"I guess I know about myself, don't I?"

Andy thought Shelley was sounding childlike. But she would not agree with Penny Vanderark. She knew that if she could only find the exact right words or offer the right kind of silence, Shelley would start facing her unhappy situation with the same kind of grown-up strong spirit she had shown when she faced — well, when she knew she had to learn the piano practically overnight and did it.

"Maybe you don't. Let us help you feel better, Shel. The whole dorm is so sorry the play didn't run, because everybody knows how much it meant to you. But it was the play that failed, not you. You were terrific."

"Oh, sure. Then why is my whole life over, tell me that," Shelley said. "There's no place for me to go. There's nothing left for me to do."

Andy was perplexed. "But there must be a million plays that you can do . . . what do you . . ." she said.

Shelley shook her head and went over to look out of the window, now darkening into night.

"No. It happens that my acting life is over," she said.

"Shelley, you don't really believe that," Andy said indignantly.

"Of course I do because it's true."

Andy shook her head.

"Stop, Andy. You don't know anything. I appreciate your good will, I really do, but you don't understand any of this. You can't possibly understand this kind of defeat."

Andy found herself beginning to be irritated by Shelley's nonstop self-pity over just one disappointment, even though Andy knew the disappointment was a big one.

"Come on, Shelley," she said. "I'm going to dedicate myself to dancing. I expect it to be very, very hard. Hard is part of the life, you know that."

Andy was still standing near the box of food just inside the room. Shelley had not suggested, by hand, or eye, or word, that she sit down, and Andy found that she was getting definitely irritated and that her deep reserves of sympathy were ebbing away.

"Shelley, at least *try*," she said.

"I don't want to. I'm miserable. I don't know what to do."

"Well, you can start by enjoying a chocolate doughnut, how about that?"

Shelley looked up, aware that Andy's tone had changed. She looked over at the food box, and at the flowers, and at Andy's sober face.

"Maybe later," she said.

"Okay," Andy said. She had had enough. "Enjoy it. See you around."

As she closed Shelley's door firmly behind her, Andy was too angry for tears.

CHAPTER NINE

She's been that way to all of us, Merrie. I asked her to Boston for the weekend. I thought that would cheer her up, wouldn't you think so? To be a guest of the Barretts? Oh, I don't mean that the way it sounds, Merrie. But my parents were ready to look after her and my older sister was going to be home. . . ."

It had been a long time since Jane felt the need to go to Merrie for the housemother's special brand of tea and sympathy, but Shelley was getting her down. Each of the girls in 407 was in the same state, to a different degree. Andy was split in her feelings. Half of her felt sad because she hadn't been able to help the older girl whom she had considered a friend, but the other half was still completely indignant at Shelley's rude, self-pitying behavior. It was an uncomfortable condition for the loving and giving Andy. Toby's outstretched helping hand, in the form of her offer to take Shelley out for a buggy ride, had been greeted with equal shortness.

"And guess what she told Toby," Jane said to Merrie. "She told her she didn't care to go out in any bumpy old horse-buggy of Randy's, and if she ever did want to, she could ask Randy herself because she had known Randy long before Toby ever met him. Isn't that the *rudest*?"

Merrie's lips were set in a straight line as she poured more tea for Jane and herself.

"I'll certainly speak to Shelley," she said.

"Please don't, Merrie. At least, don't do it for our sake."

Sitting on the flowered chintz sofa which matched, and faced, the wing chair on which Merrie was curled up, Jane felt, as always, comforted by the classic New England atmosphere the housemother had created.

"No, don't do it for us. We've already decided just not to bother with her any more. We all feel the same way," Jane continued. "It's not that we don't realize that she's awfully unhappy. We do. But we don't care about it the way we did before."

"I'm sorry that's true, but it's understandable, Jane. I think you girls have behaved beautifully and kindly. I'm very proud of you just as you should be proud of yourselves." Merrie paused and, without it showing, studied Jane. The girl seemed at the edge of tears. "Have another cookie, Jane. Have lots of them. I know they don't have the special power of Alison's but . . ." Merrie smiled as Jane, surprised, seemed suddenly easier.

Merrie's cookies were rich and fattening, not at all like the health food cookies that Alison used to keep on hand to give out for comfort and treats. Jane was very glad to take one and another and another.

Merrie uncurled and leaned forward.

"You girls do realize that I gave Shelley sanctuary here because she really needed it when the play closed. She had planned on being in the play all winter so completely that she simply couldn't handle the big change of plan. Ms. Allardyce — " Merrie was talking about the head mistress of Canby Hall "— has been in touch with her family, and Shelley's going to stay a while longer, until she can pull herself together and get on with her life. I think she just needs time, Jane, plenty of time. Let's give her that."

Jane nodded politely and stood up and brushed away some crumbs from her skirt. "Thank you, Merrie. Thanks very much for letting me let it out. We've all been so confused — and angry. I feel a million times better now."

"Any time, Jane. That's what I'm here for."

"Well, I'm for Merrie, if that's what Merrie said," Toby said when Jane reported back to her roommates. "As far as I'm concerned, Shelley can have all the time she wants — without me."

Andy, stretched out on her bed, arms behind her head, agreed.

"Without me, too," she said. "Who needs to be hurt like that? Besides . . ." Her voice faded off and a soft, happy smile appeared on her face.

"Besides, Matt just called," Toby said, interpreting for her roommate.

"Great," Jane said.

"It's going to be pizza and ice-skating for us on Saturday night, and I can't wait." Andy kept smiling.

"Cary and the band are playing at Jake's Joint again this weekend. I'm getting sort of weary of the place, but Cary says the acoustics are terrific so I guess I'll be with him there. How about you, Toby? Have anything special for the weekend?"

"Listen, it's only Tuesday," Toby said. "What I have is algebra homework."

Toby paused. She looked at Jane. She looked over at Andy. Toby had had a problem for over a week, and she faced the fact that so far she hadn't been able to handle it alone. Could she share it with her roommates? It was about the small packet that had come in the mail from Neal. She had been carrying it around, or leaving it under her pillow, since it arrived. The day they had planned the party for Shelley she thought she might be able to open it but finally just couldn't.

"You see, I think he's sent back all my letters," she mumbled into the air.

"Did you hear something?" Andy asked Jane.

"I *think* so," Jane answered.

Toby resolutely got up from her desk, walked to her bed and pulled the packet out from under her rainbow-patterned pillow.

"I got this in the mail from Neal more than a week ago, and I've been afraid to open it. I'm going to open it now. I don't want either of you to do anything. I just want you to be here in case I faint or something."

Toby and Andy raised questioning eyebrows to each other.

"Okay," they both said.

"Jane, remember on the bus when you made me understand about Neal and his aunt's horse, and I said I was going to write to him?"

"Sure. And I saw you doing that when we got back. You always get that certain look when you're writing to Neal."

"I'm serious, Jane," Toby said.

"It's a nice look, Toby," Jane said.

"Anyway, I did sort of apologize to him and right away he sent me" — she held the packet out for them to see — "this." She looked nervously at the packet. "I'm sure it's all the letters I ever wrote him." She looked down shyly. "He told me once that he had saved them all." Then she looked up again. "Now I have to open it. Enough is enough, right? If he's sent me back my letters . . . if he has . . ."

"Toby, *open* it," Andy demanded.

In a second, the wrapping paper was off and on the floor, and in total amazement, Toby saw that she was holding, not a pile of letters, not even one letter. Instead, Neal had sent her a book. She read the title out loud.

"*Dressage: Begin the Right Way* by Lockie Richards."

In the time it took for Andy to let out a long breath of relief, all three roommates were having another case of their galloping giggles, Toby most of all.

"Do you think Neal's trying to tell you something?" Jane asked, and that made them laugh even harder, as though it were the funniest question in the world.

"Well, now I know what I'm doing on Saturday," Toby finally managed to say.

Chapter Ten

Once more on an early Saturday morning, Toby and Andy tiptoed out of 407 together, leaving Jane sleeping in her bed, and once again they separated to go to their favorite extracurricular activities. Andy went eagerly to her Advanced Dance Class in the arts building, and Toby for Randy's farm and a ride on Maxine. Toby had studied every page of Neal's dressage book and had decided that as long as she was going to Randy's anyway, she wouldn't mind getting better acquainted with the horse Barnaby.

As she rode along on the bus to the farm, Toby found that phrases, pictures, and odd facts were sticking in her mind from Neal's book. The most surprising fact, she decided, was that a Greek named Zenophon wrote a book about how to train and ride a horse as long ago as 400 B.C.

She also decided she could probably pick

up the technique of riding dressage without too much trouble, even though it seemed ditsy. You were hardly supposed to move your hands, or the reins. You were hardly supposed to move your feet. When you rode dressage, the only parts of your body that you were supposed to move were ones that didn't show — hips, calves, thighs. That's what the book said, but Toby didn't quite believe it. Anyway, it was silly riding, she thought. It didn't have any purpose, like riding out to work cattle or to get from place one to place two. It was show-off riding.

Toby wrapped her long, wool scarf twice around her neck, pulled her wool cap tighter over her red curls, and huddled into her duffel coat. The air was starting to do its autumn thing.

One of the things Toby really liked about her Saturday expeditions to Randy's farm was the routine of it. Certain things were always the same. When she got there this time, hot coffee was waiting, as usual, and as usual, she wrapped her hands around the steaming mug to keep them warm. As usual, Randy took some time off from his chores to come with her into the barn where Maxine was being saddled for her. As always, Maxine nuzzled Toby's hand as thank-you for the carrot Toby gave her.

"I thought I'd take a look at that fancy

horse, Barnaby," Toby said to Randy as casually as she could.

But the stall was empty.

"He's out being exercised," Randy said.

"You mean somebody here knows how to make him move?"

"I guess I do mean that," Randy said. He gave Toby a leg up on Maxine and tipped his worn cap to her.

"Have a good ride," he said, as always, but this time with a particular half-smile that Toby did not exactly understand.

"Let's go, old girl," she said, flapping the reins against Maxine's neck, digging her heels into Maxine's flanks, talking the horse into moving out of the barn and toward the woods. As she passed the ring, the corral-like enclosure Randy had built when he started boarding a few horses, she saw a man riding Barnaby diagonally across the circle of the ring. To make the diagonal, the horse was crossing his front legs, then going straight along, then crossing his front legs again, all at a pretty trot. In the instant she noticed how straight and still the rider sat in the saddle, she realized he was Neal.

Before she had time to be upset or angry or even puzzled that Neal had come from Boston to Randy's without even letting her know, he rode over to her.

"Hi, there, my Toby."

Toby mumbled.

"If you're asking what I'm doing here, I'm exercising Barnaby."

"I can see that," Toby muttered, patting Maxine's neck in order to avoid Neal's eyes.

"He has to be exercised," Neal said.

"I guess so," Toby murmured.

"Randy said you were probably coming today. I was waiting for you to show up." Neal paused for some reaction. "Toby, cheer up, will you? Weren't you admiring my riding?"

"You look pretty good up there," Toby acknowledged.

"Did you get my present?" Neal asked.

"The book? Sure."

Why, Toby asked herself, am I behaving like a nerd? "Neal, I hardly understood a word about that dressage riding," she said. She pulled Maxine around to come closer to him. "You know what I mean? It was like I didn't know anything about riding at all."

"Want to come on into the ring and try it?"

"I'm not a hundred percent sure," Toby said, but she guided Maxine through the gateway. "Hello, Barnaby," she said, leaning over to pat the big horse. "Okay," she said, after taking more time to pat Barnaby than she really had to and only finally looking up at Neal. "Okay. How do we start?"

"Easy," Neal said, sounding very confident.

It felt odd but pleasant to Toby to be with Neal around horses, even if it was for something so new and fancy.

"For beginners," Neal said, "kick your feet out of the stirrups. You want to get a special centered sense of balance."

"Maxine doesn't have a clue what I'm doing," Toby said, laughing as she followed Neal's instructions. "But then, neither do I."

For the next twenty minutes or so, Neal demonstrated, and Toby tried to follow on Maxine, the techniques of guiding the pretty walk, trot, and canter of a dressage horse. Then they dismounted and Toby got up on Barnaby. Barnaby stood beautifully still. Neal reminded Toby to hold her hands balanced and still, then told her what to do with her knee, calf, and thigh. She did what he said, and to her great delight, Barnaby responded by starting his elegant, high-stepping walk.

"I did it, I did it, I got him to move!" Toby exclaimed — but not loudly. She knew horses had sensitive hearing. "Hey, Neal!"

Later, Toby back on Maxine and Neal back on Barnaby, they left the ring for the ride in the woods that Toby always enjoyed so much. At first almost all she noticed was how elegantly Neal sat on Barnaby. None of the easy slouch that was her way.

"You look gorgeous." She had almost said *gorg'*, almost used a Shelleyism! "But I don't think you could stay in that saddle for eight or ten hours the way cowpokes have to on their horses."

"I'm sure I couldn't," Neal said, laughing. "And anyway," he sighed, "like I told you, I don't really like riding, except with you. I just happened to be born the nephew of my aunt the horsewoman."

After that, they didn't talk about horses any more and the day ended with hamburgers in Greenleaf and a movie — and with Toby glad all over again that Neal was her boyfriend.

Toby awoke the next morning feeling fine but when she stood up and started to move around, she discovered she had a terrible stomachache.

"I don't believe this," she complained to her roommates. "I feel as though somebody strapped me in a steel corset, right here." She pressed her hands against the bottom of her ribs.

"Rise above it and rejoice," Jane said, neat and tidy in her blue robe. "This day I plan to clean up everything — my bed, the floor near my bed, my desk, and my bureau."

"How'll you know where to begin?" Andy asked.

"No problem. I'll just start at the top and work down," Jane said.

"Hey, will somebody please worry with me? I really hurt in the gut," Toby said.

"You've obviously used a new set of

muscles," Andy explained. "It happens in dance class all the time. I'm always glad when a muscle hurts the day after class. It means I've exercised new muscles that needed it."

"But I don't do anything diff — " Toby cut the word off. Of course she had done something different. She must have been using new muscles yesterday when she was trying that dressage. Did she have this dumb almost-stomachache from *riding*? "A bellyache from horseback riding. I don't believe it. Ouch," she said.

Jane really was as good as her word. She actually went to work picking up her clothes and books from the floor where she had dropped them — some yesterday, some earlier, some so long ago she had forgotten them.

"Oh, my goodness, here it is," she said, holding up a green binder that had been under two layers of jeans and one of sweaters and socks. "I did this theme for English two weeks ago. I *knew* I had done it, and you never heard as many excuses as I made to MacPherson about why I couldn't hand it in."

"What happened?" Toby asked. She had flopped back on her bed, nursing her aches.

Jane shrugged. "I had to write another one. It's all right, though. I'll use this next time."

"If you remember where you drop it," Andy said.

"I'm not going to drop it. I'm going to put it neatly in the center drawer of my desk."

Andy applauded.

"Hey, Andy," Toby said, rising slightly from her bed of pain. "I saw you and Matt in Greenleaf yesterday evening. With your ice skates over your shoulders. You looked like one of those happy TV commercials."

"Yep. That's us. A happy TV commercial. But I didn't see you, Toby. Where were you?"

"Oh, Neal and I were in line at the movies, across the street."

"Neal? A reconciliation?" Jane asked.

"Come on, Jane. As if you didn't know Neal was going to accidentally on purpose be at Randy's when I got there."

"Well, maybe he did call and ask what time you usually went over on Saturday mornings."

"Do you somehow get the idea of conspiracy, Andy?" Toby asked.

"Only the most loving and concerned kind, Toby," Andy answered.

"Talking about seeing somebody walking along — " Jane interrupted herself as she uncovered and held up a crumpled red shirt. "Isn't this yours, Toby?"

Toby looked up. "It sure is. My favorite from-home shirt. I've turned out my bureau drawer three times looking for it."

Jane tossed the shirt to Toby. "It's interesting to discover what's been lying down here all this time," she said.

"Oh, don't make me laugh," Toby groaned. "I hurt too much."

Jane made compassionate sounds. "Poor Toby. Anyway, as I was saying, *I* saw somebody walking along yesterday, too. At the lioness. When Cary came over, he wanted to rub the ear for luck. Some booking agent or something was going to be at Jake's Joint to listen to the group. Big doings. Well, while we were there, Shelley came through the grove.

"Shelley who?" Toby asked.

"Toby! Was she rubbing the ear, too, Jane?" Andy asked.

"Nope. She just walked in and walked by. I didn't say hello because I thought she ought to first. And she didn't."

There was a silence in Room 407.

Jane went on picking things up and putting them away from around her bed, so her pale blue and pink rug, the bed itself, and the nearby chair appeared in view for the first time since the term began. "I think I'll clear the desk tomorrow," she said finally and flopped down on the bed. Toby lay on her rainbow comforter and stared up at her tea bag. Andy, in blue tights and a super-large green sweatshirt, started doing bends and stretches and turns, softly humming the theme from the ballet *Giselle*.

"It's terrific to have the whole floor of the room again. I forgot we had so much space," she said and began to do little high leaps in a small circle.

Soon she was dancing in a larger circle, happily doing her small high leaps past Jane's bed, around Toby's, and past her own. Her roommates watched her circling the room, admiring her as they always did when she burst forth into spontaneous dancing. Andy made a leap and a graceful landing, a leap and a graceful landing, a leap and — instead of the graceful landing, Andy suddenly fell hard. She had fallen many times before but this time was different. Before the girls could gasp, Andy heard a crack and felt a terrible pain in her right foot. And instead of getting up, she lay unmoving on the floor, staring in agony at her foot. Toby jumped up and went to her. Jane ran out of the room, through the hall, up the stairs.

"Merrie, Merrie," she cried out. "Come quickly. Andy's hurt."

Chapter Eleven

Toby and Jane were waiting in the lounge area off to one side of the hospital emergency room, sitting on bright blue chairs. Across from them the chairs were yellow. At the side, they were sharp green. On the wall of the doorway, at a distance, the girls could see blue, yellow, and green lines leading inside. They didn't know which color the nurse had followed when she pushed Andy's wheelchair through the door and out of sight, Merrie alongside, holding Andy's hand.

"They try to make it look cheerful, I guess," Toby muttered.

The emergency room of the Greenleaf Hospital was surprisingly large, well-organized, and busy — perhaps because Greenleaf had a number of schools, including Canby Hall and Oakley Prep.

But waiting in even the most efficient, fancy, well-arranged, colorful lounge of an emergency ward of a hospital, worrying about your roommate, your friend, was awful. The girls couldn't look away from the entrance door that kept swinging open to let in a frightened mother with a sick baby in her arms, an elderly man bent over and groaning and supported by a man and a woman, a frightened-looking boy accompanying another boy who had a bleeding knee. Nurses, doctors, aides, kept scurrying around. The girls wondered what was happening with Andy.

"Listen, she probably just sprained a toe or something like that," Toby said.

"Maybe."

Jane was still seeing the ashen look of Andy's face on the drive to the hospital. Merrie had driven carefully, but as fast as possible, and Andy had cringed with every tiny bump.

For a terrible while, Jane wondered if she had been responsible for Andy's accident. If she hadn't cleared up the floor space near her bed, Andy might not have been dancing so exuberantly. That's dumb thinking, she told herself immediately, and Andy would be the first one to say so. Andy was always dancing, or twisting, or moving around in her special graceful way. It didn't matter that there was more space in the room. It wasn't anybody's fault. That's what Jane told herself over and over again as they waited, but she couldn't stop wondering.

"What do you think they're doing in there?" she asked Toby.

"I would think they're taking Xrays, And, you know, when things aren't really serious, they let you wait and all that. I mean, that boy who was bleeding all over the place, they'd make sure Andy's okay but then they'd probably take care of him first and let her sit around."

"Maybe," Jane said.

"That's what I think, anyway."

Finally — it felt to Toby like hours later — Merrie came to the doorway and waved to them to come in. Andy was there sitting in a wheelchair. Her foot was enclosed in what looked like a gigantic cast and the nurse's aide behind the chair was carrying crutches.

"That looks impressive," Toby said.

"Is everything okay?" Jane asked.

The group got larger. A tall, young doctor with a surprising streak of white running through her otherwise dark hair and a warm, weary smile joined them and put a large envelope of Xrays in Andy's lap.

"Here are your pictures, Andy. Keep them safe."

"I will," Andy said, looking up at her with a small smile.

"Well, one of us will," Merrie said.

Andy looked drawn and still a little frightened but the girls knew she was going to be all right by the relieved expression on Merrie's face.

"Your friend has a small broken bone in her foot but she should be fine in no time," the doctor told Toby and Jane. Then she turned to Merrie. "All right, she can go home with you now, but keep her in the infirmary, off that foot."

"We'll look after her."

"We've been in touch with the school doctor. He'll come over to see her tonight."

"Thank you, doctor," Merrie said.

"And don't worry. It's a fracture but it shouldn't create any special problem. It'll heal in its own time." Then she turned to the patient. "Good-bye, Andy," she said. "Be very easy on that foot and it'll be fine."

"Okay, doctor."

The aide wheeled Andy out of the emergency room. They settled Andy in the passenger seat of Merrie's car. Toby and Jane got in the back, taking charge of the crutches.

"She's going to be all right. The doctor says so," Toby announced.

Room 407 was having a succession of girls arriving, even though it was after Lights Out.

"How's Andy taking it?" Maggie Morrison asked.

"Well, she won't be able to dance for a while, no question of that. And she's scared," Jane said.

Jane sat cross-legged on her bed, right on the quilt. There was no in-between layer of anything like jeans, sweaters, dresses, coats, any of the clutter that used to be there.

"You don't look so hot yourself," Maggie said.

"I feel knocked out. I mean, Andy's all tucked in. Guess who actually tucked her in, by the way."

"Merrie Pembroke. Give us another," Dee answered.

"Wrong," Toby said. "P.A. was waiting at the infirmary when we arrived."

"Hoo-ha," Dee said. "Patrice Allardyce, the headmistress herself!"

"And she was very nice, too," Jane said.

"Well, is it a real break? I mean, a bad break?" Maggie persisted. "Is she in a cast?"

"She's got crutches."

"Hey, Jane, you *do* look terrible," Dee said.

"It's been a long day. I'm pretty tired," Jane said, starting to get undressed and ready for bed. She pulled off her sweater and dropped it on the floor, undid her jeans and kicked them to the end of the bed, tossed her underwear wherever it fell. She took her long sleep sweatshirt out of the bureau drawer where she had so carefully folded it away earlier in the day and put it on. Then she decided she wanted to wear pajamas instead so she got out a pair of pink flannel pajamas with flowers and threw the sweatshirt on top of the sweater on the floor.

During the week, visits to the infirmary were Number One priority on the agendas of Andy's roommates. Visiting Andy was also high on the schedules of almost all the girls in Baker House as well as Andy's many friends in her various ballet classes and elsewhere at the school. Merrie checked in every day, often with her delicious cookies.

When Ms. Allardyce had come again to see the patient first thing in the morning after the accident, Andy's room still looked hospital-neat and respectable. But after a few days, the white walls were covered with splashes of color — bright cards and funny handmade get-well messages, long and short, including a funny poem by Penny Vanderark, who was an aspiring writer like Jane. Penny had illustrated it with almost every possible color Magic Marker. Assorted toys and other silly presents and perfume and books filled even more space.

"Oh, Jane, I don't really deserve all this attention," Andy protested when Jane dashed into the infirmary between classes and presented her with a big white stuffed teddy bear.

The bear had dark blue eyes and a neatly stitched little red nose and a line of a mouth that some sewing genius made look so adorable and ingenuous that when Andy set it up next to her, it seemed to be looking at her with all the eager sympathy a live puppy would have.

"We miss you! How do you feel, Andy?" Jane asked, not even taking time to sit down.

"I'm great. My foot's not so good." Andy answered, getting skillfully onto her crutches.

Jane felt a sweep of admiration for the brave front her roommate was putting up.

"Oh, Andy," she said.

"I'm terrific, honestly." Andy laughed as she maneuvered to a chair and lowered herself into it.

Andy started to put the crutches next to her chair. Jane hurried to help, but Andy thanked her and took care of them herself. She put them neatly within reach.

"Does it hurt a lot, Andy?" Jane asked sympathetically.

"Oh, sure, it hurts a lot, but I'm not *suffering* with it, Jane," Andy said. "You know, there's a difference between having some pain and having some pain and thinking it's the end of the world. There's a *big diff'*, as you-know-who would say."

"We've forgotten Shelley," Jane reminded her.

"Right. I forgot!" Andy shook her head. "Dopey Shelley."

"Yeah. She's still around. We see her sometimes with Merrie, but I don't know what she does with herself."

"Shelley really surprised me so much," Andy said.

"I think it's simple," Jane said. "She's just

completely and totally self-centered, that's all. You, on the other hand — "

"I'm the heroine of the world, right? Jane, I wasn't kidding about not suffering. I'm not saying I like this" — she lifted and wiggled her injured foot a little and winced — "but hurting yourself is part of a dancer's life."

"That sounds terrific," Jane said meaning exactly the opposite.

"You expect it and accept it. I learned that when I was about ten years old. I wouldn't know myself if I didn't have pains and soreness most of the time."

"Masochism," Jane said.

"No. Just the truth. But I'm ready to get out of here. The doctor says over the weekend, and Ms. Johnson agrees."

Ms. Johnson was the new R.N. in charge of the infirmary and a combination of ogre and caretaker at one and the same time.

"That's great. Listen, Toby's bringing over your mail later today, and I think there's a package from your family so you shouldn't be too hungry tonight. . . ."

"Good. I'm having company," Andy said. "Matt and I will pig out."

"I guess you *are* definitely okay," Jane said.

"That's what I told you," Andy said.

"I think it's coming along pretty well, don't you?" Andy said to Ms. Johnson later, when the nurse came to restrap the foot. "When do I get to use it?"

Ms. Johnson ran her hand expertly over Andy's arch, toes, the sole of the foot. "Does it hurt here? Here? No? That's good. Yes, it seems to be healing just fine. You'll be seeing the doctor tomorrow, and I'm sure she'll be very pleased."

Andy got up and hobbled around the room without the crutches.

"Feels okay," she said. But soon she sat down again. "This has always been my problem foot. It always sort of wants to go its own way. I don't know whether that's from structure or muscle. I sprained it roller-skating when I was a little kid, and I always thought it must have healed funny. Is that possible?"

"Don't you worry your head about it," Ms. Johnson said.

"Like I was telling Jane, dancers get to know their bodies pretty well," Andy said.

"Is that so?" The nurse wasn't used to fifteen-year-old girls being so coolly analytical about such things.

"You know what I've had with that foot, in only seven years of ballet dancing?"

"No, I don't."

"Well, outside of that sprain roller-skating, which doesn't really count, I've had ingrown toenails, blisters, pulled muscles, muscle spasms, tendonitis. . . ."

"And now a little broken bone," Ms. Johnson said.

With the strapping in place, Andy tried a

few movements, raising her leg, wiggling her foot a little.

"Careful, there," Ms. Johnson said. The phone rang and Ms. Johnson answered it.

"It sounds like a boy, Andy," she said.

Andy grinned and picked up the phone. Ms. Johnson waved and left the room.

"Ms. Johnson said it was a boy," Andy said into the phone.

"I heard her. That your nurse?"

"Not *my* nurse, Matt. The nurse for the whole infirmary. Of course, it so happens that I'm the only one in the infirmary at the moment. Are you coming over?"

"I'm practically outside the door."

"I'll be glad to see you."

Andy had been pushing back the bad thought from the moment she heard that awful crack when she fell. It was true, what she told Jane — it was a dancer's fate to get hurt and be sore and all of that — but there was something about the pain in the arch of her foot that made her feel the injury might be more serious than anyone was telling her. She wouldn't mind any foot injury, as long as it got better, as long as she could still dance. What if she couldn't dance again? That was the bad thought. But the doctor said it was going to be just fine.

"Matt? I'll be so happy to see you," she said.

Chapter Twelve

In the mail slot for Room 407 was the customary letter from Andy's parents. Toby weighed it in her hand and once again wondered what it must be like to receive big fat letters three or four times a week every week from your family. She heard from her own father regularly. Every ten days he wrote her a terse half page or so.

Toby knew her father cherished her. Since her mother died five years back, he had been both parents to her, and she and he were good friends as well as loving father and daughter. But, Toby thought, putting Andy's mail in a separate pile that she would take with her to the infirmary, they didn't exactly share the warmth and exuberance that produced all those letters from the Cord family to their Andrea.

Andy's parents' latest package had arrived, too, and was waiting on the hall table. It seemed double the usual size, if that were possible. Toby wondered for a moment whether the Cords had finally managed to ship hot ribs. She even put her hand flat against the corrugated box to feel for warmth. No luck. Ever since Ms. Allardyce had called Andy's family to tell them about Andy's accident, assuring them it wasn't serious — and after they had spoken to Canby Hall's doctor who had added reassurance — Andy's father, mother, both older brothers, and her baby sister as well had been burning up the phone lines between Chicago and the Canby Hall infirmary. But phone contact with Andy was not enough for the Cord family. The CARE packages were like the family's hands-on contact with their beloved daughter and the packages that had arrived since the accident were enormous.

The dorm doorbell rang and Toby answered it.

"Delivery for Ms. Jane Barrett."

"I'll take it," Toby said.

The UPS man gave her a form to sign, then handed over a heavy dress-sized box, an awkward narrower long box, and a strong square box. Mrs. Betts, who was passing and had a friendly interest in everything about the girls at Baker House, immediately made note of the sendee, which was the same on the boxes.

"Look at that, dear," she said, pointing to the address label. The label said the packages came from "Miller's, East Rutherford, New Jersey," The two l's in the word "Miller's" were formed by drawings of high riding boots.

"Oh, Jane," Mrs. Betts said as Jane, coming back to the dorm after classes, nearly bumped into the departing UPS man. "These are for you."

Jane took the boxes from Toby and made a quick note of the Miller's labels.

"No! It was supposed to be a surprise."

"What was?" Toby asked.

"Looks as if Jane's joining you in horseback riding, Toby," Mrs. Betts said.

"Does it?" Toby asked, looking questioningly at Jane.

"Thanks, Mrs. Betts," Jane said.

"What, dear?" Mrs. Betts said.

"Gosh, Tobe, the whole thing's gone wrong. These are from Neal. I was supposed to hide them until he said it was okay."

"You're not making a fantastic amount of sense, Jane."

"Oh, come on upstairs," said Jane.

Merrie was coming downstairs and Shelley was with her. So was a handsome older woman both girls recognized instantly as Lorraine Moss, the actress they had met at the opening night. "You remember Jane Barrett and Toby Houston. . . ." Merrie made introductions.

"Of course." Lorraine Moss smiled warmly

at the girls. "You're Shelley's friends, the girls who live in her old room."

The girls avoided looking at Shelley but they could almost sense, as though it were a physical thing in the air, that she was embarrassed and sad — and unfriendly. Jane, already fumbling with books, notebooks, satchel handbag and three bulky boxes, now also fumbled with words.

"Um, yes, well, we . . . how nice to see you."

Toby simply nodded how d'ya do.

"Ms. Moss has a train to catch," Merrie said, as though explaining that they had to rush away.

Watching the three backs going down the stairs, Jane made a little grimace. "Well, well, what do you think of that?" she asked.

"Maybe she came to haul Shelley out of here," Toby remarked sourly.

"I don't think so," Jane said.

"I don't care."

"It isn't really exactly the same for you, Toby. You didn't ever actually like Shelley. That's why I thought it was terrific of you to try to cheer her up with the buggy ride."

"A lot of good it did."

"Yes. Funny how a seemingly nice person can turn out to be so mean," Jane agreed. Then she laughed. "But listen, if I'm ever that far down in the dumps, feel free to make me the same offer. I love buggy rides."

* * *

It had only been eight days since her clean-up and Andy's accident, but Jane's area of Room 407 was again a grand mess. When she and Toby got into the room, she dumped her books on the floor and swept her bed clear of its jumble of everything. Then she put the largest box on the bed and tried to open it. Her fingers didn't work. She found a pair of scissors and soon was blithely tossing away layers of tissue paper and, finally, item by item, drawing forth a dazzling collection of riding clothes. Toby almost couldn't believe her eyes.

First came bright white breeches, with suede stitched on them not only at the knees but also around the seat. That was followed by a long formal black three-button jacket with slits at the sides. After that — it was as though the box were bottomless — appeared a white cotton collarless shirt with two separate neck bands that seemed to fasten at the ends with Velcro. There was also a stiff white cotton scarf and a pair of black leather gloves that were ridged on the palms and reinforced oddly around the first finger and had tucks all along the wrist.

"It's very important to wear the right gloves," Jane said.

"I bet," Toby said quietly. 'I can't wait to see what's in the other boxes."

Jane opened them quickly. From the square

box came a hard round-topped black velvety-looking cap which made Toby's mouth fall open in astonishment, and from the narrower box, long, lean black leather boots so beautiful they made her mouth clamp closed again.

"Well?" Jane said.

"Well what?" Toby answered, frozen in her carefully relaxed position at the end of Jane's bed.

"Well, don't you want to put them on?" Jane asked.

"Doesn't *who* want to *what*?"

"Toby, don't be dense," Jane said. She didn't feel completely comfortable. She had told Neal she wasn't sure outfitting Toby for dressage riding was exactly the thing to do. "They're yours. They're a present from Neal. They're to wear when you — " Jane was going to let Neal do the talking about the possibility of Toby's actually showing the dressage horse in a horse show. "They're for when you ride Barnaby."

"I don't believe this," Toby said. She gazed at the assembly of clothes laid out on Jane's bed. "You remember me?" she asked. "I'm your western roommate. I'm the one who wears chaps over jeans when she's got real riding to do." She picked up the hard black velvet cap. "I wear a sun-bleached, beat-up old cowboy hat when I need something on my head. This thing?"

She plopped the cap on top of her curly red

hair and picked up and put on the jacket, too, over her crew-neck faded green sweater.

"Looks great," Jane exclaimed.

Unsmiling, Toby went to the mirror on her bureau. She examined herself front view, turned sideways, examined herself over her shoulder, turned front again, and stood looking for a long time. Soberly, she flecked an invisible speck of thread from the shoulder of the jacket. She tapped a loose fist against the hard top of the hat and studied herself some more — the elegant black jacket over her comfortable old sweater, her freckled, blue-eyed, lean face surmounted by the incongruous formal black hunter's cap. Jane watched nervously. Finally Toby spoke.

"This is just the funniest, most *eastern* thing I ever saw," she said. She shook her head in disbelief. "How could you think . . . how could you dream . . . how could you imagine . . . ?" She shook her head again and smiled and gave Jane a big hug. "Neal and you are both *crazy*," she said.

Vastly relieved, Jane started to breathe again. "I didn't know the things were going to come so quickly," she hurried to explain. "You can't imagine how I sneaked around getting the right sizes for everything. I mean, I hope I got the right sizes. I checked your jean jacket for size and then I wasn't sure a riding jacket would be the same size as a . . . and the boots? Remember the other day when you were looking for your fancy boots? Neal had them. Miller's had to be sure of your calf size for the dress boots, even though they're a million times different from cowboy boots. And . . . oh, Toby, try everything on."

Toby, laughing, nevertheless shook her head. "I'm going to tell you a secret, Jane."

"You are?"

"I think Neal is the most terrific guy in the world and when it comes to roommates, to *friends*, they don't come better than you. But about these things . . . ? You're both . . ."

"Let me guess. Crazy?"

"Yep. Oh, all right, okay, why not. I'll try them on. You understand they go right back where they came from afterwards."

"Sure, sure," Jane said.

Toby got the giggles when she was finally completely dressed in the fancy clothes. Jane had done wonders. Everything fit. Toby couldn't believe Jane's tying the scarf in double knots — it wasn't called a scarf, it was called a stock, Jane explained — and arranging it exactly so around Toby's neck and in front. The jacket hung a little loose, but that was all right. The breeches were made from a stretch fabric and fit fine. The only item that didn't make Toby laugh was the pair of boots. After she had wiggled into them, they felt terrific, she admitted to Jane. They came to her knee and they were a whole great new sensation.

Jane wanted to call all of Baker House to see how terrific Toby looked, but the minute she started for the door, Toby simply began to take the clothes off, first the jacket, then . . . Jane forcibly stopped her from unknotting the stock.

"At least show Andy," Jane pleaded. "She'll love it."

Toby hesitated.

"I'll go with you."

"Well, I *was* going over there, to see her, and bring her her mail and all."

"It'd be great, Toby. Honestly, you really do look fine. Look at yourself in the long mirror."

Toby went to the long mirror.

"Do you know that my own father would not recognize me? And if he did, he wouldn't believe what he was seeing."

"Yes, he would, Toby. Let's go see Andy, okay?"

"Well . . ." Toby drawled out the word. "It would certainly give her a laugh."

"You know it."

"Only thing is, I won't walk across campus looking like this."

"Don't worry. I'll protect you," Jane said.

They tried three coats, the longest in the closet, and settled on Toby's unending slicker. Jane hid the cap under her own coat. The evening was shining clear but when Toby went into it, carrying Andy's mail and the

CARE package, she blithely pretended it was raining out.

Andy loved the riding clothes. She made Toby turn around, walk back and forth, put the cap on, take the cap off. Matt told Toby she looked like the fanciest ad in the fanciest magazine he could think of, which made Andy laugh and Toby blush. It was clear that Andy remembered Toby's calling her and Matt a TV commercial and had told Matt and Matt remembered it, too. Andy, the strapping on her foot much reduced, hobbled gracefully around the room, even doing a small spin on the good foot, and when it came time to open the CARE package, they were all full of high spirits and good cheer. None of them would have believed that their fun wouldn't last forever.

CHAPTER THIRTEEN

Hey Neal,

As I told Jane, being a Bostonian obviously does something to the head. All the fancy duds arrived. Jane says your sister is about the same size I am, so thanks very much and please tell your sister (Jane happened to mention that your sister has a million blue ribbons for riding!!!!) that she's got some cute stuff coming to her. I have to say my daddy wouldn't let me accept a present that must have cost you as much as a good horse anyway. Are you coming to see Barnaby any time soon?

Love,
Toby

Dear Neal,

It sort of worked and sort of didn't.

Love,
Jane

Each of the girls in Room 407 was busy at her desk. Toby was thinking as she finished her note, put it in its envelope, and sealed and stamped it. She was supposed to be thinking about English, her least favorite subject, but instead she was thinking about Max, her horse at home, and this new world of riding she was being dragged into. The muscle pains had long since gone away, but she had a sinking feeling that if she went back onto Barnaby, she'd be aching and paining all over again. Not that she hadn't had a couple of painful spills, even broken her arm once, with Max. But riding Max was natural territory for her. Max was company out on the range. His four legs were almost Toby's own strong legs. They were partners. This other stuff, with Barnaby, was different. There was something challenging about it. It was so . . . she tried to find the right word. It was disciplined, that's what it was. And new to her. She had always thought she knew all she needed to know about riding horses. She sure knew everything there was to know about a western horse.

But . . . but . . . wouldn't it be a hoot to learn this dressage stuff and go home, maybe this coming summer, and try to teach it to old Max? Recalling what Neal's books had said, Toby reached for it, on top, not below, the book she had to read for English, and turned a couple of pages until she found what she had remembered reading. A horse didn't have to have "perfect conformation," the book said. Toby thought of her wheel-barrow Max. She read on, ". . . anyone, with patience and the ambition to improve their horse, can understand and execute dressage." Old Max didn't need improving, Toby thought, but it sure would be fun to teach him to do all those fancy steps and to sit there on top of him looking as though she wasn't moving a muscle. She could just imagine her dad watching. And Abe!

Thinking of home, Toby sighed. Then she came back to the here and now, sighed again, and reached reluctantly for her English book.

Jane was working on a history paper. She hoped to get it finished before going over to see Andy, but she didn't seem to be able to keep her mind on it. The evening before at the infirmary had been like a party, the three roommates — Toby all dressed up — and Matt. Jane bit the end of her pen. Matt, she decided as she always did when she thought about it, just couldn't be a nicer guy. He and Cary, even though they both went to Oakley Prep, weren't very much alike. Cary was always so Carylike and Matt — well, Jane faced the fact that it must be tough sometimes to be one of maybe half a dozen black guys at Oakley. She could imagine Matt years and years from now, out of Harvard Law School, cool and smooth and on top of things. That's how Matt would be.

Jane knew Andy glowed when Matt was around, even if Andy didn't realize it. That was what really mattered. Andy. I'm lucky to know Andy, Jane mused. That she liked her roommate went without saying. But she also admired her so much.

Jane tried to imagine herself with a broken bone in her foot, tried to imagine Andy's feeling that, okay, that's how it was when you wanted to be a dancer. Jane couldn't do it. She just couldn't imagine herself being as brave as Andy. She looked down at the paper she was writing. It said History 5 at the top, and her name, and the rest of the page was blank.

Andy, alone in her room at the infirmary, was trying to concentrate on her history textbook — she had to keep up with classroom work as much as possible, and Dee and Maggie had just come by with her history reading assignment, and some dance friends came by, too, with chatter and laughs and a pretty little bunch of flowers. When they left, Andy had conscientiously opened the book to the right page and was seriously reading about the great American Marshall Plan for Europe after World War II. It was important, and there would be tests on it, probably even with essay questions. Her interest and attention, Andy finally admitted, were about zero. After she read the same paragraph three times and still didn't know what it was saying, she put the book down and looked around her infirmary room.

The scrubbed wood floor reminded her of nothing except a studio, empty and inviting. Andy started wiggling her toes, the ones on the good foot and those of the foot with the silly broken bone. A little twinge. It was healing just fine, exactly the way the doctor said it would. She got up from her chair and reached for the crutches, then decided to see what happened without them. She stood on both feet for a moment. Then she lifted her arms, and the full stretch felt comfortable. Slowly, she bent over, testing her balance. She had to flex the knee on the leg with the bad foot, and the foot itself protested slightly, but only slightly. Encouraged, she started a small, simple dance step. She gently arched the foot with the broken bone. And stopped. She could not do it. She tried again and again stopped. It wasn't just pain. And it wasn't just that the foot would not arch. Andy was suddenly deeply afraid.

Something inside her told her that the bad thought had become reality.

Toby and Jane went to see Andy that evening after homework and before dining hall. Both girls really thought Andy ought to be back with them, but the doctor said no, and Ms.

Johnson said no, and Ms. Allardyce said no, and Merrie said that another few days and the stairs would be no trouble for Andy to go up and down, and Andy also would be well enough to protect herself from the dorm action. "Whatever *that's* supposed to mean," Jane said.

"Wow, this air tonight really feels like pin-pricks, doesn't it?" Toby said. They were crossing behind the dorms to the infirmary in a darkening evening, bundled against the sharp, clean air. "Like tiny knives almost. You know, Jane, I think autumn is my favorite season up here. Listen to those leaves crackle."

There was a streak of sensitivity in Toby that always delighted Jane when it showed. Jane liked the sight of the nearly bare trees they were walking past and the sound on the crisp fallen leaves under their feet but she was so used to them she didn't always see or hear them. Toby always seemed to notice.

They went into the infirmary, waving to Ms. Johnson at her desk near the entrance and going straight to Andy's room, all ready with smiles, mail, and a report on what Gigi Norton had said to. . . .

But once there, they were astonished to find Andy lying on her bed absolutely inert and staring into space instead of sitting up and waiting for them, full of her natural verve.

"Andy. Are you okay?" Toby quickly asked.

Andy slowly turned her head on the pillow to look at Toby. Then she turned back and stared again at nothing.

"No," she said.

"What happened, roomie?" This was Jane, coming closer, reaching for Andy's hand.

"Nothing."

"Andy!"

The girl on the bed made a slight, sickly sound that might have been a laugh.

"Nothing," she said again. "Only I'll never be able to dance again."

"Who said so?" Jane demanded indignantly.

"Nobody has to tell me. I know it."

"What do you mean?" Toby said. "Hey, Andy, that's not what the doctor said."

"She doesn't know my body the way I do. I tried. I know. I can't dance."

It was shocking to Jane and Toby to see Andy knocked out. Andy was the one of the three girls in 407 who always was *up*.

"But you aren't over your accident, yet," Jane said. "You have to start exercising again, and go slowly at first. All that kind of thing. You have to give yourself time, Andy."

"I know about that. And it's not a matter of time."

"Hey, Andy, come on, kid," Toby began, and while she was talking, Jane slipped out of the room.

Ms. Johnson wasn't at her desk. She wasn't in her office. Finally, Jane found a door marked "Private," probably Ms. Johnson's own room, and knocked on the door.

Ms. Johnson came to the door. She had taken off the uniform she always wore — white pants, white overblouse, pearls around her neck, little pearl earrings — and was wearing a good-looking red wool bathrobe and leather slippers.

"Oh, Jane." Ms. Johnson apologized for her costume. "I thought that while you girls were here keeping my patient company, I'd have my shower. I know, I know. Most people bathe in the morning or at night but I always like to take my shower and dress before dinner."

Jane registered the bathrobe, but her mind was on something else.

"I thought the doctor said Andy's foot was healing perfectly," she said accusingly.

"Why, yes, of course," Ms. Johnson agreed, "it's healing very nicely."

"Are you sure?" Jane answered.

"I am, yes. If Andy does her therapy exercises regularly, she should be fine, permanently. Now, we don't know, yet, that she'll be able to be a professional dancer as she seems to want to be, but — "

"*Seems* to!" Jane exclaimed. "There's nothing else in the world she wants."

"People sometimes change their minds about their careers, Jane."

"Andy won't," Jane insisted.

"Maybe not." Ms. Johnson shifted her

weight, looked with concern at Jane. "My dear," she said, "foot bones are very tricky, but as far as I know, from everything I've seen myself and everything the doctor has told me and told her, Andy should be as good as new. And very soon, too."

"It's just that she doesn't seem to think so, Ms. Johnson."

"Really?"

"I mean, she is *down*."

"Is that so? She was fine when I saw her an hour or so ago."

"Well, she isn't now, Ms. Johnson."

The nurse hesitated only one split second. "You go on back to Andy, Jane," she said briskly. "I'll be there in a minute."

Jane let out her breath. She hadn't been aware she was holding it in. Ms. Johnson's general air of efficiency and ability and concern reassured her.

"Okay, Ms. Johnson," she said and hurried away.

When she got back to Andy's room, nothing was different.

"Andy, I just saw Ms. Johnson. Nobody but you seems to think you won't be able to dance."

Andy shook her head. "Nobody but me has to think so, Jane." She lifted herself up on one elbow and sadly looked at her two close friends.

"Too bad, isn't it?" she said.

Jane looked at Toby and Toby looked at Jane.

"Andy, come on," Jane almost pleaded. "This isn't like you. Where's the Andy that was telling me all about pain but no suffering?"

"I don't have any pain in my foot," Andy said falling back on the bed, in a voice that sounded dead. "Not real pain. A twinge. That's all."

The rest was unspoken. Both girls knew their wonderful roommate was suffering intensely.

"Andy?" Toby decided to try funny-shock to see if that would rouse her. "Hey, Andy, here's your mail. Some of it's terrific. The catalogs, you know, like we all get? Look at this one. It's a catalog from a place called Norm Johnson. It says you should, and I quote, 'escape from the ordinary.' You can get sheepskin covers for the seats of your car or a complete wildflower meadow by mail. Which do you want?"

Andy didn't respond.

"I've always wanted a wildflower meadow," Jane said, trying to help fill the silence.

"Me, too," Toby said weakly.

Suddenly the door of Andy's room opened.

"Well, now, what's this, Andy?"

Ms. Johnson's bright voice was in sharp contrast to her appearance. Jane gasped in surprise. Ms. Johnson had exchanged her trim red robe for an incredibly sloppy old chenille robe. She had put her short straight hair into big pink curlers that went this way and that way all over her head and had slathered cold cream on her face. Ms. Johnson, who was the neatest, tidiest person in all of Canby Hall! Andy was so startled she gasped and covered her mouth with her hand.

In words and manner, the nurse acted as though she were still in her trim white uniform. She went straight to Andy on her bed.

"Well, now, you're not feeling so good, is that it, dear? Let's see if there's any temperature, shall we? Open your mouth," and from the recesses of a pocket of the terrible-looking robe, Ms. Johnson pulled out a thermometer case, picked up the thermometer, shook it, and stuck it under Andy's tongue. With her hand on Andy's pulse, she gazed at the two other girls with a blithe, breezy, seemingly distracted little smile that confused them both. They wanted to laugh, but you didn't laugh at Ms. Johnson.

Andy, meanwhile, her mouth closed over the thermometer, gazed at Ms. Johnson, rolled her eyes questioningly toward Jane and Toby, looked back at the nurse. She wiggled her foot, Jane noticed. After Ms. Johnson took the thermometer out of her mouth and was busy looking at it, Andy roused herself enough to smother hidden giggles with her friends.

Ms. Johnson put the thermometer away, bent to test the strapping on Andy's foot, looking carefully at Andy as she did so, and finally pulled a chair over and sat down by Andy's bed, completely attentive.

"I think you girls can go to dining hall now," she said, still being efficient, still looking ridiculous. "Andy and I are going to have a nice long talk and settle the problems of the world."

Andy gave them a relaxed "Isn't she nuts!" grin and shake of her head. She seemed *almost* restored to herself, "which," Toby and Jane agreed as they made their way across campus to the dining hall, "was Ms. Johnson's whole idea in the first place."

Chapter Fourteen

On Saturday, Toby felt sad when she slipped out of Baker House alone. She missed Andy.

She felt sad all the way to Randy's where she hoped she could get rid of some of the unhappiness by getting on a horse. Poor Andy. How miserable it must be to be so miserable! Ms. Johnson's technique had worked — but not for long. The day before, when Toby and Jane visited Andy, she was, again, down in the dumps.

"How's Andy?" Randy wanted to know first thing when Toby arrived at the farm.

"Not so good," she had to say.

They went together toward the barn, warming their hands on their coffee mugs.

"But I thought everything was okay."

"It was. The doctor says it still is. It's just that Andy doesn't believe it."

"How come?" Randy asked.

Toby shook her head. "It's really tough,"

she said. "When she had the accident, she was terrific. In great spirits, you know? She made me ashamed of my hollering about my muscles after riding Barnaby. Her only complaint was that they were taking too much care of her, fussing too much, making her stay in the infirmary too long."

"They can't be too careful, Toby. They're responsible for you kids."

"Yeah," Toby said. "But Andy said they were on overkill. She was really cheerful, Randy, and doing all the things she was supposed to — exercises, you know — until just a couple of days ago. Now she hardly does anything. She doesn't talk much. She just broods. She says she can't dance. The thing is, she doesn't *try* to get better so she *can* dance. That's what's got everybody worried."

"Poor kid," Randy said.

"Absolutely," Toby agreed.

They were nearing the stalls, and as Barnaby heard them, or smelled them, pass by, he turned his beautiful calm face toward them.

"Sorry, Barnaby," Toby said. "I could only get hold of one carrot today and that's for Maxine." She turned to Randy. "Who's exercising this fella?"

"Good question," Randy said. "It's a problem. He really needs a workout every day. We've been taking him out and having him go through his paces at the end of a long rein."

"Is that what Neal's book calls *lungeing*?"

"Yes, I think so. Neal showed us how to do it. It works okay and Barnaby's okay."

Toby paused. "That's good," she said. She paused again. "As long as he's okay."

Randy made one of his mumbling agreeing noises as they walked past Barnaby toward Maxine's stall.

"Do you know if Neal is coming here this weekend?" he asked as they watched Maxine being led out.

"I, uh, no, I don't happen to know," Toby said.

"Last time he called, he didn't think he could make it but he wasn't sure."

"That so?"

"He's concerned. He says his aunt will probably kill him if her horse isn't in prime condition when she gets here."

"When's that going to be?"

Randy laughed. "That's the hard part. Neal doesn't know."

Toby looked at Maxine. The stable boy was just tossing her saddle on her back. She'd love to ride like the wind on Maxine, gallop out on the paths in the woods. Then she looked back at Barnaby's stall where Barnaby was still quietly, intelligently, curiously looking out after her and Randy and the activity around Maxine. Then Toby sipped her coffee and gazed deep into the mug, as though she were trying to read her fortune in the coffee. Finally she was ready.

"Hey, Randy?" she began.

"Yep?" he said.

"About Neal. . . ."

She had thought hard about Neal. She didn't know if she would ever be able to make up to him for her behavior when he first brought her out to meet Barnaby, but she wanted to try. She owed him. She knew she never was going to ride Barnaby in any horse show. But she knew Neal was right. Anybody who could ride the way she could, like part of the horse, could learn dressage.

"Randy, how about seeing if I can put Barnaby through his paces?"

"How, Toby? Neither of us knows the fine points of dressage."

Toby drew out of her jacket pocket the thin book on riding that Neal had sent her. "I just happen to have here — "

"You just happen to?"

They both laughed.

"Listen, Randy. It's a very complete book. We can work from it. You just tell me what it says to do, and I'll do it — I'll try to do it. Then you look at the pictures and tell me if he looks right. There are lots of pictures. You'll be able to see if I'm working him right or wrong."

"Whoa, there," Randy said. "Barnaby's no toy to play with."

"I know that," Toby said indignantly. "I

also know, and so do you, that I'm a very good rider, and I'm not going to hurt that horse."

"Maxine's waiting for you, Toby."

"Yeah, I thought I wanted to take her out today. But Randy, I can change my mind. Barnaby's only here because Neal thought I'd like to ride him, and neither of us wants Neal to get into trouble and . . ."

Randy took the book and looked through it for a while. He got caught and read one page, then another, then another a few pages along. "Interesting," he said.

"How about it? I mean, ah, Randy, why not?"

Randy grinned his crooked grin at her and signaled the stable boy to unsaddle Maxine and put her back in her stall.

"Why not indeed? I'm not sure this is going to work, Toby, but okay, let's find out."

Toby told a long and funny story of her adventures on Barnaby when she got to the infirmary that afternoon. She made a melodrama of how Barnaby had kept trotting and trotting and trotting when she wanted him to stop or how Randy kept shouting, no, no, you're doing it backwards — nothing that Toby tried seemed to get through to Andy. A whole group from Baker House was there and they laughed encouragingly but Toby's stories fell flat. It was apparent that the old ways were no good for this new Andy.

After everybody else left, Toby and Jane stopped talking about horses and got to the serious matter of Andy and dancing. They begged Andy, who was limping from chair to bed and bed to chair, to do *something* dancelike, perhaps point her toe a little. Ms. Johnson had said that would be a good exercise for the healing foot. After saying no, she didn't want to, and asking her roommates not to bother, even telling them they didn't *understand,* Andy hesitantly stood up and walked to the middle of the room. She was still beautiful Andy and even with a faint limp still moved more gracefully than either of the others could begin to do. As her roommates watched, Andy took a deep breath and slowly raised her arms and seemed to lift her whole body. There was a moment of expectation filling the room. Then, in an almost explosive loss of energy, Andy went completely limp. She could not make the first move to dance.

"She's so afraid," Jane told Merrie that evening. "She's afraid if she tries to take a dance step, she won't be able to do it, so she doesn't even try. It's frightening, Merrie."

Toby was with Jane on this visit to Merrie. They came for more than tea and empathy.

"We hate to see Andy so miserable, that's what it is," Toby said.

Merrie nodded. "We're all sorry about the way Andy's feeling," she said. "I can assure you that everyone's concerned. Ms. Allardyce is in constant touch with Andy and with her doctor. The doctor thinks it's a delayed reaction to the accident. You know how cheerful Andy was at first. It was very brave of her but" — Merrie shrugged — "the doctor says this is just the other side of the same coin."

"Do you agree with that, Merrie?" Jane asked and answered her own question. "I don't. Andy has convinced herself she won't ever be able to dance again. Is that just the opposite of being cheerful?"

"Maybe it is, Jane."

"Well, how long is it supposed to last?"

'I wish I could tell you, but I simply can't."

"But meanwhile, Merrie — "

"Yes, Jane, meanwhile," Merrie agreed sadly.

Toby looked at Jane and Jane nodded.

"Merrie, we had an idea," Toby said. "You're probably right that Andy'll snap back. She probably *was* too cheerful at first."

But I still don't agree with that, Jane told herself. She remembered what Andy told her about how dancers accept the fact that they hurt themselves all the time and have aches and pains.

"We decided we'd like to call Andy's family. Do you think that's all right? I mean, they might have some ideas that would help us make her feel better."

* * *

The minute they got the idea, the girls had begun collecting quarters in Jane's old oversized flowered tea cup, the one that was from her grandmother's set of china. At nine the next morning, Sunday — they wanted to call early to make sure they'd find the Cord family at home — they scooped up the quarters, counted them out, knew they had more than enough to call Chicago, and went downstairs to the phone booths off the lounge. Jane had just lifted the phone off the hook when Toby suddenly stopped her.

"It's too early!" Toby exclaimed.

"It's nine o'clock. We agreed on nine," Jane said, startled.

"It's nine o'clock here. It's earlier in Chicago. Doesn't Andy always subtract an hour when she's calling her family?"

"You're right, definitely. Chicago time's an hour behind Greenleaf time."

They squeezed out of the booth and went into the lounge. Over on a side table were a pitcher of orange juice, a pitcher of milk, an urn of coffee, and plates of Danish courtesy of the dining hall. Merrie had continued one of Alison's customs, the sort-of brunch in the lounge on Sunday, with the big Boston, New York, D.C., and L.A. Sunday newspapers available to anybody who wanted to read them. The girls helped themselves and sat down on one of the sofas to be nervous for an hour.

"I didn't think Merrie was enthusiastic, did you?" Jane asked Toby.

"Nope."

"But she didn't object."

"Nope."

"We're not going to say anything to scare the Cords, are we?"

"Nope."

"Toby, I want to ask you something," Jane said. "You can eat everything they give us in dining hall, can't you?"

"Sure."

"How is that possible, Toby? Have you tasted these Danish?"

"Sure have. And I'm going to have another one, too. Sorry about that, Jane."

"Wow." Nobody had been able to figure out how Toby could love Canby Hall food the way she did.

On her way back to the sofa, carefully balancing her Danish and refilled cup of coffee, Toby stumbled against the foot of somebody deep in the Arts and Leisure section of *The New York Times*. There was a surprised squeak and a startled Shelley peered out from behind the paper.

"Oh. Toby."

"Sorry, Shelley," Toby said, juggling the coffee cup which had slipped and threatened to spill.

Will it be a conversation, Toby wondered after the cup was righted. Shelley glanced around the lounge. She saw Jane on the sofa and the space next to her that Toby was obviously going toward. She seemed to be looking for someone else, too. Andy, perhaps, Toby thought. Maybe she'll say something about not seeing Andy around. Toby waited, but the only thing that came from Shelley was a weak little half-smile. Then she retreated behind the theatrical section of *The New York Times.*

Finally, the girls were half in, half out of the booth, Jane making the call, Toby as close as possible so she could hear, and the phone was ringing in the Cord house.

"Hello?"

"Ms. Cord?"

"Yes."

"This is Jane Barrett, Ms. Cord. At Canby Hall."

"Jane? Is Andrea all right?"

"Well, uh, yes. She's fine. Her foot's almost all healed, I mean. Only she's a little . . . unhappy, Ms. Cord, and we thought — "

"Hello, Jane. This is Mr. Cord. I'm on the other phone. Did you say our Andrea is feeling blue?"

"Yes, Mr. Cord, I did. It sort of bothers us, Toby and me, and we wondered — "

"But her foot's all right, isn't it, Jane?"

"Yes, it is."

"But she's down in the dumps. I thought so.

I heard it in her voice when I talked to her last night."

"She's worried about dancing, Mr. Cord. She thinks she's not going to be able to dance again," Jane said.

"Doctor agree?"

"No, sir."

"But she thinks so."

"We can't get her *not* to, Mr. Cord, and we thought . . ."

Toby watched Jane nod and heard her say, "I will, Mr. Cord," and nod again and continue nodding as the voice on the other side of the phone kept up a steady warm hum. After a long time, Jane finally said, "Okay, Mr. Cord. Goodbye, Ms. Cord. Yes, okay."

Jane hung up and looked stunned.

"He or Ms. Cord, whoever doesn't stay to run the restaurant, is taking a plane this morning," she told Toby. "Whoever it is, they'll arrive early this afternoon. Nobody should bother to meet them. They'll rent a car. We have to get Andy a triple banana split immediately, vanilla, chocolate, and strawberry ice cream with cherries, pineapple, glazed walnuts, and real whipped cream, none of that artificial whipped cream."

"Vroom!" Toby said.

"And how," Jane agreed.

CHAPTER FIFTEEN

It was Mr. Cord who walked into Andy's room at the infirmary and, almost before Andy could get up from her chair, swept her up in an enormous bear hug.

"Andrea, baby," he said, rocking back and forth with her. "How's my honey?"

"Oh, Daddy!" Andy hugged him as tight as she could. She wished she could stay in her father's warm, protecting arms forever.

"You've been feeling bad, baby girl."

"Daddy, I really have."

"We'll see what we can do about that."

"Nothing can be done, but I'm awfully glad you're here."

Michael Cord pulled back a little and put one hand gently against Andy's cheek.

"Let's take a good look at you, Sweetie."

Andy raised her eyes to her father's. It was so good to see him! He looked, as always, big and warm and kind and loving. Andy smiled to see that he had worn his brightest red bow tie. She was sure it was meant to cheer her up.

At the door, Jane and Toby stood waiting and Ms. Johnson joined them. Mr. Cord had met the girls at Baker House and, with their guidance, immediately driven the short distance past the headmistress's house, along the tennis courts to the infirmary. He hadn't wanted to waste one minute. Now, after looking searchingly into his child's face, he gave her another great hug and the warmest, sweetest smile that Jane thought she had ever seen anybody give anybody. Andy was smiling tremulously, as though she were close to tears. Then, with his arm around Andy and hers around him, her father turned to the others.

"You must be Ms. Johnson," he said to the nurse. "Andrea wrote me about your being very kind to her — and making her laugh."

Ms. Johnson smiled.

"You mean my costume the other night? Well, between you and me, sometimes a little laugh is good medicine."

"I appreciate all you've done for my child," Mr. Cord said.

"She's a lovely girl, and I've enjoyed knowing her," Ms. Johnson said, beaming at Andy.

There was a pause. Mr. Cord was obviously shocked at what he had seen in Andy's face and glad that he had come and glad, too, about what he had brought with him.

"Now look here, children," he said, his arm

still tight around Andy's shoulder. "I believe in first things first, don't you? I know you, and, of course, Andrea's told me a lot of things about all of you and one of the things that I understand has been very important is the matter of sending hot barbecued ribs through the mail. It doesn't work. However . . ." he paused, "if you'll go fetch two packages you'll find on the back seat of the car, I'll let you guess what might be in them."

The girls vanished.

Mr. Cord looked at his watch and then at Ms. Johnson.

"It is about supper time, isn't it, Ms. Johnson? Andy, if it's all right with Ms. Johnson, maybe we could have a little ribs party."

Ms. Johnson immediately nodded approval.

"Jane and Toby are already here. Ms. Johnson will you stay?"

"I'd be delighted."

"Is there anybody else you'd like to ask, from your dorm?"

Andy felt as though she had just been swept up by her father again, this time by the force of his familiar vitality. "Maggie and Dee," she said. "They live next door from us in the dorm. And maybe Matt can get away from school. Daddy, did you really bring hot ribs from Chicago?" Andy asked.

"I sure did," her father said.

Mr. Cord and Ms. Johnson exchanged glances over the top of Andy's head. The girl clearly was pleased, but they both recognized that the special exuberance Andy always emanated was definitely missing.

Jane and Toby returned from the car and soon Mr. Cord had turned Andy's infirmary room into a version of the Cord family restaurant in Chicago. From one of the two big packages the girls brought in, he took out a red-checked tablecloth. With a grand flourish, he draped it over the desk. He then transformed the desk into an inviting buffet table, complete with a pile of red and white checked paper napkins, a stack of plastic plates, six-packs of soda, and food — an enormous white thermal container that opened to reveal still steaming slabs of barbecued spare ribs and other containers that held barbecue sauce, cole slaw, and french fried onions. There even was an empty red plastic container for bones. He also brought forth a large flat box with an outsize apple pie in it.

In bewildered but familiar amazement, the girls watched Mr. Cord in action. Whenever they tried to do something useful for him, he had already done it. During their last Christmas vacation, Jane and Toby had visited Chicago to help Andy help her father when the Cords faced an emergency in their restaurant. On the day after Christmas, their most reliable waitress and waiter had unexpectedly run away to elope when the restaurant had banquets scheduled for every night until New

Year's. The girls had pitched in despite Mr. and Ms. Cord's doubts, and it had been an education for everyone. Mr. Cord and Ms. Cord were warm, loving parents but they were also skilled restaurant owners. The quick, efficient way Mr. Cord was arranging this feast they were about to have reminded them of those days at the restaurant.

As Mr. Cord conferred with Ms. Johnson about cooling the soda, Andy came up to her friends.

"I think I have you to thank for this nice surprise," she said.

"We called him, Andy, I confess we did. But coming here was your father's own idea."

"I should have recognized his touch when you brought me that banana split."

"You were amazing, Andy. I never saw anybody eat one of those things in the morning," Jane said.

"It's an old magic trick of mine, Janie. Few others can master it."

"Oh, Andy, it's great to see you smiling," Jane said.

"It's going to take me a while, Jane. I'm just finding out that sometimes you can't do what you planned to do, that's all."

"Andy, stop it. You're a dancer. Your foot's okay. You'll always be a dancer. You just won't try."

"Why try something when you know you won't be able to do it?"

"Are you still Andy, or have you become somebody else?" Jane asked sadly.

"Cool it," Toby said. "Company's here."

Maggie and Dee arrived and two seconds later, Matt's car tooted out front. Matt always announced himself with two short toots, two long toots, two short toots.

It was almost impossible to believe that Mr. Cord had carried on the plane from Chicago enough ribs to satisfy the appetites of five girls, one boy, one nurse, and one father, but he had. And the ribs were delicious.

"Mr. Cord, this is terrific," Matt said. "These may be among the best ribs I ever tasted."

"Well, thank you, son."

Mr. Cord's astute dark eyes had been studying this young man his daughter liked. He saw a good-looking boy with trimmed-back hair and a tentative first mustache. Mr. Cord's hand unconsciously smoothed his own thick black mustache. Matt had dressed very carefully for this meeting with Andy's father — corduroys, a big sweatshirt faded just the right amount, Adidas, and red socks — and it was all right. Mr. Cord approved of him.

But Andrea's father was interested most of all in his daughter. He could hardly believe that what her friends had told him about her was true.

"Andrea," he said. "Will you do your — what's the name of that dance you always do around the dining room table at home? The one where you swing your skirt and twirl and snap your fingers? Isn't it called the tarantula? No, that's a spider."

"The dance is a tarantella, Daddy. But I'm afraid I can't do it any more."

"Sure you'll do it again, baby," he said.

"No, I won't Daddy. It's okay. I have to be realistic. I'm beginning to get used to the idea that I won't be a dancer. There are lots of other things a person can do. I'm almost as efficient as you are, Daddy. I can work with a dance company. They always need managers and things like that. Just because I can't dance any more — "

"Andrea, nobody but you says you can't dance."

Andy didn't answer.

"You've just got something stuck in your head, Andrea. Here, let me give you a good shake and get it out of there."

"Daddy, please."

"I want to see a tarantella before I leave here."

"That'll be a long time, Daddy. Mother will miss you."

"Now, Andrea, you know what I mean."

"Oh, Daddy."

"No, I've never seen our Andrea like this before," Mr. Cord said.

He was sitting slumped in one of the big

chairs in the lounge near the doorway. Matt had gone back to Oakley and Dee and Maggie, after many thanks, had excused themselves. Jane and Toby were sitting there with him. So was Merrie.

It was close to Lights Out time and only a few girls were still downstairs, wandering through the lounge. The last Ping-Pong players in the game room had put their paddles away — the click-click of the Ping-Pong ball had been a soft background sound in the lounge — and went through on their way toward the stairs; a few other girls passed by on their way to the snack machines; one girl crossed over to the phone booth.

Nobody heard Shelley come in from a long, lonely walk around the campus. They were too absorbed in their conversation to see her stop with surprise when she saw them, an unexpected foursome — Merrie, two of the three girls from 407, and a troubled-looking man whom she recognized from one of Andy's photos. She quickly realized he must be Andy's father. But why was he here? Where was Andy?

Shelley stepped back and listened.

"Maybe I should just pick the child up and take her home," Michael Cord was saying.

"Oh, please don't do that, Mr. Cord," Toby said.

"I'd vote against it, too," Merrie said. "The doctor says Andy doesn't have to stay in the infirmary after tonight. As you know, she believes Andy can manage the stairs just fine now, and I think Andy'll feel much better once she's back with her friends. I certainly think we should give that a try."

"Well, I don't know. It's the darndest thing. Andrea is not a girl to give up, and now it seems that's just what she's done."

"If she'd only *try*. All she has to do is arch her foot once and I bet she'd be dancing in a week," Jane said. "The broken bone in that foot is supposed to be all healed now."

Shelley Hyde felt as though a sharp cold knife had just gone through her. She suddenly felt the shock of how self-absorbed she had been ever since the play closed. She had half-noticed that Andy didn't seem to be around much but that hadn't mattered to her. Nothing did but her own unhappiness. She hadn't thought about anybody but herself for much too long, she realized. Now there was someone else she wanted to think about. Quietly, so none of the group in the lounge would hear her, she opened the door of Baker House and carefully closed it behind her. Then she went quickly to the infirmary.

CHAPTER SIXTEEN

When Ms. Johnson tapped on the door, Andy was sitting in a chair looking out into the night with only one small lamp breaking the darkness of her room.

"You have some more company, Andy," Ms. Johnson said standing at the door. "I told her it was late, and you might be in bed . . . which I see you're not, dear. But she seems very determined. She absolutely insists on seeing you."

"Who is it, Ms. Johnson?"

"She says to tell you Shelley Hyde and that she must see you, please."

"Shelley? No interest, thank you."

"I've already asked her to come back tomorrow, but she's very persistent."

Andy just shook her head, no, but almost in that same moment, Shelley appeared.

"Please let me come in, Andy," she said. "Don't be as awful as I've been."

Andy was quiet.

"It's up to you, dear," Ms. Johnson said, looking from her patient to the patient's visitor, ready to remove Shelley instantly if Andy really wanted her to.

Andy hesitated. It had been a heavy day, and she didn't need any more problems. But Shelley obviously, finally, had something to say to her.

"It's all right, Ms. Johnson. She can come in."

As the nurse left, a slightly quizzical expression on her face, the room suddenly was brightly lit. She had switched on the overhead light.

"Ms. Johnson likes it to be bright," Andy murmured.

Shelley took a few steps into the room, loosened her coat and waited.

"It's hot in here," Andy said, not sullenly but not cordially either. She could not forget the hurtful brush-off Shelley had given her and her friends.

"It does seem a little warm."

"You can take your coat off," Andy said, offhandedly gesturing toward the old-fashioned brass coat rack standing in a corner.

Shelley quickly took off her long pink jacket and crossed the room to hang it up. She still dressed in her own bright, unique style, Andy noticed, sneaking a glance at her visitor. Shelley was wearing dark red sweats, pants and top, and pink sneakers. Her face seemed paler than Andy remembered, and she almost seemed to have hollows in her cheeks. Not that Shelley could really look gaunt. Her round face was too wide and open for that. Shelley turned back and seemed to take a deep breath. Andy waited.

"I was out for a walk this evening," the older girl began. "I've been doing a lot of that, walking by myself around the campus."

Andy didn't say anything. Was she supposed to feel sorry for Shelley?

"When I went back in to Baker, I saw your father in the dorm lounge, with Merrie and your roommates. They were talking about you. What's wrong, Andy?"

"Nothing."

"It's something. That's why you're in the infirmary. Your father was talking about taking you home — "

Andy reacted to that. "I won't go home," she said indignantly.

"But Merrie advised against it, and your roommates certainly want you to stay. What happened, Andy?"

Andy wiggled in her chair for a moment, trying to settle the thoughts that were jumping around in her head.

"What difference could it possibly make to you, Shelley?" she finally said.

"I want you to be okay."

"I'm just fine, thanks." Andy didn't want to

give in to the concern she saw that Shelley really felt.

"You're right to be angry. I've been behaving like a spoiled brat. I've been moping around in that princess's room as though I were a princess myself, a princess who has lost her whole kingdom."

"Shelley, puh-leese."

Shelley stopped immediately.

"You're right. I'm dumb. It's just that I'm so ashamed of myself that I don't know what to say so I'm saying nonsense. Please tell me what's with you, Andy. I have an idea we can help each other."

"Shelley, when you were in pain, I tried to help you. Do you happen to remember that?"

"Yes, I do."

"Are you *pozz*?" Andy asked, deliberately using a Shelleyism.

"I'm *pozz*. What can I say? If my mother knew how rude and unkind I've been to you and Jane and Toby and almost every single person at Baker House and the whole school, she'd — "

Andy didn't want to listen. She was tired. She was uncomfortable.

"*Really?*" she said.

"Andy, believe me. I don't think there's any point in my saying I'm sorry and expecting you to forgive me. Why should you? I've been too selfish too long for that. I'm here for something else. You. Now, did I hear Jane say you broke a bone in your foot?"

"A small bone in the arch," Andy muttered.

"Oh, not good for a dancer."

"I'm not going to be a dancer."

"Because of the broken bone in your foot?"

"Of course."

"Let me see if I can read the script. You've been here in the infirmary for . . . how long?"

"Long enough. I go back to the dorm tomorrow."

"And all that time, while the bone's been healing probably ten times stronger than it was before, you've been sitting around thinking, I can't dance anymore, I can't dance anymore, I can't dance anymore."

"Maybe it's been something like that."

"And everybody around has been telling you your foot will really get well and you can dance on it . . . with it."

"Maybe."

"But you don't believe them because you know. You know how you feel. You know your body."

"That's absolutely right, so there."

"Andy, it's absolutely wrong. I heard what they were saying in the lounge where there was no reason to try to hide anything to make you feel better. They weren't worried about your foot. They were worried about *you*. Your foot's really all right. Oh, you'll have to work to get it limber again, but what's a little work to a dancer? It's the way you feel that's wrong. You still have your terrific dancer's body. You still have all your talent. I'm sure your ambition is still burning even though one piece of temporary bad luck has you convinced that there's no point in being ambitious. Andy, the reality is that you — " Shelley stopped herself midsentence. "Hey, do you hear what I'm saying?"

Shelley had such a surprised expression on her face that Andy laughed out loud.

"You have to tell me who you were talking about," Andy said, still laughing.

"But that's *terrif*," Shelley said. "I'm talking about both of us, aren't I?"

She got up from the edge of the bed where she had been sitting and started to walk up and down the room.

"But it can't be true of me. I did fail as an actress. I had a chance and I failed."

Andy shrugged. "That man, Michael Moore, your company manager at the theater, he said you had everything going for you to be a success."

"Michael Moore said that?"

"Didn't he tell you, too?"

"I guess I didn't hear him," Shelley said slowly.

I guess there were things that I didn't hear, either, Andy thought. "Maybe I haven't been so smart after all," she said, half to herself, half out loud.

Shelley looked sharply at her and then walked briskly to the coat rack, took her coat, and put it on. "I'm off now, Andy."

"Oh!" Andy was surprised at the abruptness.

"I'm enough of an actress to know my cue to exit," Shelley said. Then she laughed. "We're a great pair," she said. "I came over to help you and it looks as though I cured myself. So long, Andy. Good luck."

"Take care, Shelley," Andy said.

After Shelley left, Andy sat for a while in her chair in the quiet, empty room. She looked at her foot thoughtfully. Then she slowly stood up and stepped away from the chair. Carefully she put her weight on her left foot. Slowly she lifted her right leg and foot in its furry red slipper. With a small, neat swing from her hip, she sent the slipper flying across the room. Here goes something, she said to herself, and arched her bare foot and took a dancer's step on it. She wobbled and quickly put a hand on the back of the chair for support.

I guess it's not going to happen too quickly, she thought, unexpectedly short of breath. It'll probably take ages. She flexed and unflexed her foot. "Wow, it's like a board," she said aloud, but a lightness, a happiness was winging through her.

* * *

The next morning, Monday, there was a flurry of activity around the infirmary. Mr. Cord arrived bright and early, determined to take Andy back with him to Chicago, but instead found Andy packed and ready to go back to Baker House. She only had a small overnight bag for clothes, but in addition, there were all the toy animals, cards, and silly presents she had received, and they made a large bundle. It took a split second for Michael Cord to realize that Andy was her old self again and that the only way he could possibly separate her from Canby Hall was to tie her up and carry her away kicking and screaming. He would have minded the screaming but not the kicking. Andy wasn't frightened about her foot any more.

"Oh, Andrea, my good girl, good morning to you," he said.

"Hiya, Dad. Hey, Dad, could you drive me and this junk over to the dorm?"

"I might be able to do that. Are you all ready?"

"Yes, I am."

"Well, then" — Ms. Johnson came out to the car with Andy — "Ms. Johnson, we give you our warm thanks and say good-bye."

"I'm so glad, Mr. Cord. Good-bye. And Andy, dear, good luck."

Andy hugged Ms. Johnson and then literally hopped into the car with her father.

"Poor foot isn't used to my making demands on it anymore. This is its last free ride," she said and was delighted when her father laughed in appreciation of her terrible play on words.

It was only a short drive on the campus road to get to the dorm, but Andy used every minute of it.

"Dad, I can't thank you enough for coming here. It was so terrific to see you. You're the world's greatest father, you know that? And the ribs! They were sensational. It was so terrific of you to bring them and all the fixings and everything. You liked my friends, didn't you? They're nice, aren't they?" She grinned over at her father. "Matt's nice, isn't he?"

"Very nice, Andrea."

"Do you know that I have to go to classes today? Check in at Baker and zoom right across to History. About time I came back, isn't it? Don't tell anybody, but I can't wait. Getting assignments and doing homework alone in that infirmary is blahsville. I've got a million messages for you to please take home, Dad. Give Mom a big kiss and tell her . . ."

Andy didn't stop until the car pulled up in front of Baker House. Merrie came out to meet them.

"At last, Andy," she said.

* * *

That night in Room 407 the roommates had a gala reunion. Andy had been welcomed back in classes, in the halls, in the dorm, but this was special, just the three girls alone together again. With food, of course. They had just come from dining hall so they weren't what they could call *starved,* but when Ms. Betts said there was a delivery for 407 and it turned out to be banana splits for three, they all dug in. Andy, who had crawled into bed — she still had some strength to get back — shook her head.

"It's not just that my father is a great chef and knows everything about food. He also performs miracles. I can't even imagine how he managed this." She pointed to the ice cream, only beginning to melt deliciously.

"Don't forget he brought us hot ribs. After that, anything's possible," Toby said.

Andy breathed a great sigh of contentment.

"I feel I've been in another country for a hundred years," she said. "What's been happening?"

Jane, sitting on the floor in her blue zippered robe, put down her banana split to give full attention to her answer.

"Well, do you remember I said I was working on this impossible history paper?"

"Act as though I don't remember anything," Andy said with a flush of embarrassment.

"Gee, Andy," Toby said.

"It was on the Marshall Plan after World War II. I almost understand the Marshall Plan and I got an A."

"You did not, Jane," Toby said. "No false modesty. She got an A+, the only one in the class."

"Great," Andy said. "I was trying to read that assignment. Boy, do I have catching up to do. How about you, Toby? When are we going to see you on that fancy horse in that fancy riding outfit?"

"Never."

That startled Jane so much she coughed on one of the glazed walnuts.

"What?" she exclaimed.

"That's right. Saturday I packed up those white breeches and that nutsy hat and all that stuff and mailed it back to Boston."

"Wait a minute, Toby. I thought you were enjoying riding Barnaby on Saturday."

"So did I," Andy said. "You made it sound as though you were really having fun when you told us about it at the infirmary."

"Well, no reason not to have a couple of laughs, but no, on Saturday I found out just how I feel about dressage. I gave it my all on Saturday. I finally got the hang of it, too. You just use your weight differently, you shift more, you guide the horse more with your seat and your legs and thighs than with your hands and feet. It's a different way of riding. And it's great, don't misunderstand. But it's not *my* way. It never will be. I don't want it to be."

"Have you told Neal that?" Jane wanted to know.

"Not yet."

"I can't wait till he finds out. His aunt's coming up pretty soon and if you don't show Barnaby at that county horse show, she'll probably make him do it."

"We'll all go watch," Andy declared.

Toby laughed. "I have to write Neal a letter," she said.

"Okay. What else?" Andy asked.

"Well, we have this roommate who broke her foot and — " Toby began. But she was interrupted.

"I don't believe this," a voice said. "It's exactly what we used to do."

They looked up and Shelley was at the doorway, in a down coat and woolly hat, a valise in her hand.

"I came to say good-bye to you," she said.

A brief silence fell.

"Where are you going, Shelley?" Andy asked.

"Home," Shelley answered. "Then back to college. I can face it now. Andy, I can't tell you how grateful I am to you."

"Shelley! You saved *me*."

"I guess you could say we both couldn't face the next step."

"But you were very cruel, Shelley," Jane said coolly.

"Yes, I was. And to say I'm sorry doesn't begin to tell you how I feel. I'll be sorry about the way I acted here . . . well, I'll never forget it, I promise you."

"Okay, Shelley," Andy said.

"There's something else I want to say — I *am* going to be an *actresssss!*"

"And *I'm* going to be a dancer," Andy said with a smile.

"Right! And there will be other disappointments. There always are in the theater and in everything, I guess. But I'm sure I'll handle them differently from now on. I'll never be as awful to anybody as I was here with you. I hope you'll all forgive me."

Andy got up out of bed and went to Shelley. She held out her hand.

"I forgive you, and thank you, Shelley. Good luck."

What started as a handshake ended as a hug. Jane and Toby came to the door, too, to say good-bye.

"Before I leave, though, there's something very important I have to know," Shelley said. She paused, her eyes twinkling.

"No, I won't tell you what the tea bag means," Toby said.

"Yes, you'll always be welcome in Room 407," Jane said.

"What do you want to know?" Toby asked.

"You see, I've been eating at Merrie's all this time," Shelley said. "Tell me, is the dining hall still serving that marvelous gourmet food?"

For a moment, the girls looked blank. Then they burst out laughing and assured her it was.

"Are you *pozz*?" Shelley asked. She smiled, a little tearfully, Jane thought, and picked up her valise and left.

Toby closed the door, Andy started collecting the banana split containers, and Jane took them from her and put them in the wastebasket.

"Get to bed, Andy," she said. "You have to be tired."

After Andy obediently climbed back under her comforter — she *was* tired — she sat up and looked at the two other girls.

"I want to make a speech," she said.

Jane and Toby gave her their full attention. "I think you two are the most terrific friends a person could possibly have. Even when I was acting as terrible as Shelley — "

Toby interrupted. "Which was never, Andrea Cord. Don't think it."

"Well, it wasn't easy on you anyway, and you were great. And my whole speech is, thanks, friends."

As Andy snuggled under her comforter and Jane and Toby got ready for bed and Lights Out, their hearts felt warm with the feeling of friendship and harmony and love and respect that filled every corner of their room, Room 407 Baker House, Canby Hall.